Ralph Sadler

The Book of Ayub

Known in the west as Job

Ralph Sadler

The Book of Ayub
Known in the west as Job

ISBN/EAN: 9783337219598

Printed in Europe, USA, Canada, Australia, Japan

Cover: Foto ©Andreas Hilbeck / pixelio.de

More available books at **www.hansebooks.com**

THE BOOK OF AYUB:

KNOWN IN THE WEST AS JOB.

Ye have heard of the patience of Job.—JAMES V. 11, A.V.

Beloved, think it not strange concerning the fiery trial which is to try you, as though some strange thing happened to you.—I. PETER IV. 12, A.V.

Let thy gold be cast in the furnace,
 Thy red gold precious and bright;
Do not fear the hungry fire
 With its caverns of burning light,
And thy gold shall return more precious
 Free from every spot and stain.

In the cruel furnace of sorrow
 Cast thy heart. Do not faint nor wail,
Let thy hand be firm and steady;
 Do not let thy spirit quail,
But wait till the trial is over
 And take thy heart again.

PREFACE.

It is very difficult to write any sort of preface or introduction to the book of Ayub. It is written in the tersest and most condensed style, without a superfluous word, and makes tremendous demands upon any one who attempts to give an English version of it. That all its difficulties are solved in the rendering now offered, the translator does not pretend to claim ; he can only say that he has made great endeavours to follow the thought of the writer through his often enigmatical language, and if he has not always been successful in this, he has at least arrived at a very much better understanding of the book and its writer while making the endeavour. Many passages which are simply unintelligible in our previous English versions yield a plain and intelligible sense enough when every word is given its true root meaning, and due regard is given to the continuity of the thought and the general plan of the book.

The castrophe, however, is not a little remarkable, and has been greatly obscured by the fact that a large part of what appears in our English versions, as referring to Leviathan, is really a description of man ; though the subject does not appear to have recognised his own portrait, as seen from without, and sketched for him by a master hand. From chap. xli. 17, to the end of the chapter, Man is the subject of the speaker. The Septuagint translator so understood the passage, and though the language is highly enigmatical, still the plain rendering is MAN SHALL CLEAVE TO HIS BROTHER, and unless man be in some sense the subject the catastrophe becomes unintelligible.

Ayub had been complaining that he could not get a hearing; but when at last the Almighty intervenes, He does so to plead His own cause, and demands that Ayub shall answer Him. "Wilt thou condemn Me that thou mayest be righteous?" Chap. xl. 8 A.V. And He concludes His speech in fact by complaining that Ayub is too proud to speak to Him. And so Ayub understood what he heard, as his reply makes clear. It was not the Almighty who was the source of his troubles and trials, and even the jealousy and enmity of Satan would have had little or no power if he had not found men willing instruments in his hand; first to destroy and carry off his property, and afterwards to ply him with counsels of despair. Man in fact has not yet learned his power, and constantly allows himself to become a tool in the hands of his mortal foe to his own injury, and that of his brother man. "When he arises the gods will give way; they will be broken and miss the road."

R. SADLER.

Hail, smiling Morn, that tip'st the hills with gold.
Whose rosy fingers ope the gates of day;
Who, the gay face of Nature dost unfold,
At whose bright presence darkness flies away !

THE BOOK OF AYUB.

I. THERE WAS A MAN IN THE LAND OF UZ, Ayub by name. And this man was whole-hearted and straightforward, one that feared the gods and turned aside from evil.

2. And there were born to him seven sons and three daughters; and he had acquired seven thousand sheep, and three thousand camels, and five hundred yoke of oxen, and five hundred she-asses, and his servants were multiplied greatly; and this man was renowned among all the sons of the East.

3. And. his sons went and kept open house each his day, and sent and called their three sisters to eat and drink with them. And when the days of feasting had gone about, Ayub used to send and cleanse them. And he rose early in the morning and offered burnt-offerings commemorating them all; for Ayub said, Perchance my sons have done

---

1. *Ayub;* the name is still in use in the East. Ayoub or Eyoub Khan is a name well known in Affghanistan.

Whole-hearted; as a noun the word means *integrity, wholeness;* the opposite of double-minded, see James i. 8.

2. *Yoke;* or *pairs,* two oxen being a yoke of oxen.

3. *Open house;* or more literally *drinking house.*

Burnt-offerings; this seems the intention, though the word is applicable to anything offered on an altar.

amiss and been guilty of presumption. Thus did Ayub regularly.

5. And the day arrived for the sons of the gods to go in and present themselves before Jehovah, and Satan also went in in their midst.

6. And Jehovah said to Satan, Where have you come from? And Satan replied to Jehovah and said, From a tour on the earth, and from walking about on it.

7. And Jehovah said, Didst set thy heart on my servant Ayub? For there is none like him on the earth, whole-hearted and straightforward, god-fearing and turning aside from evil.

8. And Satan replied to Jehovah and said, Doth Ayub fear the gods for naught? Hast not Thou made a fence about him, and about his house, and about all that belongs to him on every side? The works of his hands thou hast blessed, and his cattle are spread abroad upon the earth.

---

4. *Done amiss;* the word has precisely the sense of the Greek ἁμαρτάνω, *to fail, miss the mark.*

Been guilty of presumption; or literally *have blessed* (patronised?) *Aleim in their hearts.* The nature of the failure Ayub feared was evidently lest they had been too contented and happy in the exuberance of the good things of this earthly life, and so shewn contempt for the Unseen.

5. *The sons of the gods;* or *the sons of Aleim.* Evidently the intention is to represent a reception held for the younger members of the host of heaven. Satan is represented as a young heaven-abider who had not learned manners and abuses the notice accorded him by the King of heaven in the manner described. It seems better to retain the word as a proper name than to translate *the obstructor,* or, as some explain it, *the traveller.* Whether the name represents an individual, or any one who takes the part of accuser, is really of no importance. Christ stands as the Advocate of mankind, to plead the cause of those who appeal to Him against all and sundry.

Fear the gods; the point here is that Satan, one of the sons of the gods, disavows any special admiration for Ayub, on the grounds that it is prompted by self-interest. In fact, he says it is no wonder if Ayub reverences the gods, seeing how high he stands in the favour of their King.

But stretch forth now thy hand and touch all that he hath. Will he bless thee to thy face?

9. And Jehovah said to Satan, Lo all that is his is in thine hand, only upon him stretch not forth thy hand. And Satan went forth from the presence of Jehovah.

10. And the day came when his sons and his daughters were eating and drinking wine in the house of their eldest brother; and a messenger came in to Ayub and said: The oxen were ploughing and the she-asses were grazing beside them, and Sabæans fell upon them and seized them, and the servants they slew with the edge of the sword; and I only am escaped, I alone, to shew it thee.

11. While he was yet speaking another came in and said: The fire of God fell from heaven and set on fire the sheep and the servants and devoured them; and I only escaped, I alone, to shew thee.

12. While he was yet speaking another came in and said: Chaldæans formed three bands and swept down upon the camels and took them, and the servants they slew with the edge of the sword; and I only escaped, I alone, to shew thee.

13. While he was yet speaking another came in and said: Your sons and your daughters were eating and drinking wine in the house of their eldest brother, and lo, a great wind came from the side of the desert and smote on the four sides of the house, and it fell on the young folk and they are dead; and I only escaped, I alone, to shew it you.

8. *Will he bless thee to thy face?* Or it may be rendered also: *Lo, he will not bless thee to thy face.* A.V. renders *not bless* by a single word, which is at least an honest and straightforwad if not a very delicate way of turning the difficulty. R.V. shirks it altogether. The real point seems to be that Satan sees that the Almighty cannot submit to be patronised by Ayub; but he had yet to learn that Jehovah does not lack resource, and can deliver those who trust Him.

14. And Ayub arose and tore off his clothes and cut his hair close, and fell on the earth and prostrated himself, and said : Naked I issued from my mother's womb and naked I shall return thither ! Jehovah gave and Jehovah has taken. Blessed be the Name of Jehovah. Through all this Ayub was not found wanting, nor did he ascribe unsavouriness to the gods.

II. AND THE DAY ARRIVED when the sons of the gods went in to present themselves before Jehovah, and Satan also entered among them to present himself before Jehovah.

2. And Jehovah said to Satan : Where have you come from ? And Satan replied to Jehovah and said : From a tour on the earth, and from walking about on it. And Jehovah said to Satan, Didst set thy heart on my servant Ayub ? For there is none like him on the earth ; a man whole-hearted and straightforward, god-fearing and turning aside from evil. And still he holds fast his whole-heartedness, and you incited me against him to eat him up without cause.

3. And Satan replied to Jehovah and said, Flesh does after its kind, and all a man has he will give to save his life. But put forth, my Lord, thine hand and touch his bone and his flesh. Will he bless thee to thy face ?

2. *Eat him up ;* or *devour him greedily, i.e.,* to behave to him like a lion or tiger, to treat him as the god of this world treats men when he gets the chance. See I. Pet. v. 8. and many passages in the Psalms.

3. *Flesh does after its kind.* There can be little doubt that this is the meaning. The word means *skin,* and is used of the body.

Skin as skin, i.e., after its manner. For this use of the particle see Gesenius' Lexicon.

My Lord ; the particle has much the force of *now* used in entreaty, *I beseech thee,* &c. But used to a superior it is often simply honorific. See Gesenius.

4. And Jehovah said to Satan, Lo, he is in thy hand. Only respect his life. And Satan went forth from the presence of Jehovah and smote Ayub with bad ulcers from the sole of his foot to the crown of his head; and he took him a potsherd to scrape himself, and he sat down among the ashes.

5. And his wife said to him, Dost thou still hold fast thine whole-heartedness? Submit to God and die. And he said to her, As it were a word of disgrace hast thou uttered. Nay, shall we accept prosperity from God and not accept adversity? In all this Ayub sinned not with his lips.

6. And Ayub's three friends heard all the misfortunes that had befallen him, and they came each from his home; Eliphaz the Temanite, and Bildad the Shuhite, and Zophar the Naamathite, and they arranged together to go and bewail him and to condole with him. And they lifted up their eyes from afar and were not estranged from him; and they lifted up their voice and wept, and rent each his clothes, and sprinkled dust on their heads towards heaven. And they sat down beside him on the earth seven days and seven

4. *Respect;* or more literally *preserve, guard, i.e.,* do not injure.

5. *Submit to;* the word is the same as that translated *Bless* before and commonly so rendered. Properly it means *to kneel down.* The woman's suggestion was that God clearly wished to reduce Ayub to despair, which was precisely what the godling Satan did wish.

Sinned not; or *failed not.* The meaning seems to be that he refused to regard his affliction as overwhelming, or as any cause for shifting his attitude towards the Unseen.

With his lips: Oh, the power of life and death
          IN THE TONGUE!
          As the preacher saith.—ROBT. BROWNING.

6. *Were not estranged from him;* or more exactly *did not make him strange, i.e.,* they did not turn aside from him in the extremity of his affliction under his loathsome disease.

Towards heaven, in token that they shared the afflictions which had come upon him thence.

nights ; and none spoke a word to him, for they saw that his pain was passing great.

III. A T LAST AYUB OPENED HIS MOUTH and poured contempt upon his day. And Ayub answered and said : Perish the day wherein I was born, and the night which said, A male is conceived! Let that day be darkness ; let not a god from above frequent it, and let not light illumine it. Let darkness and the shadow of death claim it ; let cloud rest upon it, and let as it were the gall of days distract it.

2. Let gloom seize upon that night ; let it not rejoice among the days of the year, let it not be counted in the months of the calendar. Let that night be confusion, let

1. So far Ayub had been too overwhelmed for speech, but he had been given into the hand of Satan, who probably, thought he should find some of his friends more amenable than Ayub. At any rate he must have the opportunity of speech that the intents of his heart might be known. It is quite a mistake to suppose it wrong to curse. Fallen man in his extremity must needs execrate something. But let him direct his wrath where it is due and curse Beliar's reign and his own folly ; unless he do this he cannot be said really to desire the Reign of Jehovah. To do it is in fact to justify Him in pronouncing the curses recorded Gen. iii. 14-19.

Poured contempt upon ; In Kal Gesenius gives the meaning *to be light,* *i.e., worthless.* Here it is in Piel the intensive of Kal and evidently has a transitive force, *made exceeding light* of his day.

And the night . . . On these words Schultens says : Inducitur nox illa (in qua Jobus conceptus sit) quasi conscia mysterii et exultans ob spem prolis virilis. But this would reduce the exclamation almost to Hamlet's speech "The time is out of joint, Ah, cursed spite, that ever I was born to set it right !" Whereas Ayub seems wholly intent on his own wrongs, and not to hint in any way a consciousness that they might subserve the interests of his race.

A god ; there are gods many and lords many (I. Cor. viii. 5), although there is but One worthy of the Name.

2. *Counted in the months of the Calendar ;* the allusion is obscure to Western ideas, as we have practically only one intercalary day in four years ; but when the calendar was regulated by the moon, many intercalary days had to be interpolated to float it upon Solar time ; and these were called *silent days,*

no exultation come near it. Let those who curse the day single it out, who are eager to strip Leviathan.

3. Let the star of its dawn be dark; let it turn to the light and find none, and let it not see for the blackness of its eyelids. Inasmuch as it shut not the doors of my womb, nor hid anguish from my eyes.

4. Why did I not die from the womb, and perish from my entrance into the world? Why were there knees ready to receive me, and why breasts that I should suck?

5. For now I had been lying down and undisturbed, I had slept thenceforward and been at rest. Along with kings and counsellors of the earth, who make desolations for themselves; or with those who amass themselves gold and fill their houses with silver. Or as a failure concealed I had not been, as children that see not the light.

6. There the wicked cease to tremble, and there the mighty toilers rest. Captives are quiet together, they hear not the voice of the task-master. Small and great are there, and the slave is free from his lord.

7. Why does He give light to the wretched, and life to the bitter of soul? Who long for death and find it not, and dig for it among hidden things; who rejoice and dance in ecstasy, who are exultant when they find a grave.

and reference to them was avoided. But indeed it is well known that the dropping of three days in order to adjust the calendar, caused tremendous and most inexplicable commotion in quite modern times.

2. *Who are eager to strip Leviathan.* To seek to explain the meaning would be to number oneself among those described. But Ayub had probably read the Book of Enoch.

Anguish; properly of travail throes.

4. Ayub is not the only one who has asked such questions. Indeed in extremity they can hardly fail to occur to any thinking man. In the *Prophecy of Esra* we find precisely the same question in a more general form.

6. *Tremble;* Gesenius gives the root an intransitive meaning, to *be moved; disturbed;* and so to *tremble, quake.*

8. To a man whose path is hidden from him, and God has woven a shroud about him? For groans assail me at the sight of food, and my roars are poured out like waters.

9. For my dread and my destiny terrified me, and what I feared is come upon me. I was not secure, I was not inactive, neither did I rest; and distraction came upon me.

IV. AND ELIPHAZ THE TEMANITE REPLIED and said: If we attempt a word to you, you labour to shut our mouth with your talk. What can we do?

2. Lo, you have corrected multitudes, and strengthened hands relaxed; your words braced the tottering, you strengthened the bending knees. But now it is come upon you and you are distressed, your turn is come and you tremble.

3. Is not your reverence a confidence and strength to you, and your whole-heartedness a road for you? Reflect, I pray you, when did innocence ever perish, or when were the righteous disowned?

4. So far as I have seen, those who plough vanity and sow vexation shall reap it; from the breath of God they will perish, and by the wind of His anger they will be consumed.

8. *A shroud ;* not expressed except by implication. Ayub does not say *what* has been woven about him, he does not profess to know; but a transitive verb requires an object in English, and this word seems to give the sense pretty accurately.

9. Or perhaps, *Yet* distraction came upon me. See chap. i. 4. This seems to be the key to the whole book. Ayub had a presentiment of what was going to happen, and took every precaution he could devise to avert the wrath of the Unseen.

3. *Reverence ;* strictly *fear, i.e.,* of God according to the usual interpretation, which seems quite correct. Eliphaz seems shocked at the vehemence of his friend's words and inclined to blame him in consequence, rather than to realise the severity of the sufferings which have evoked them.

5. The roaring of a lion, and the voice of the fierce, and the teeth of the shaggy are broken; the strong one perishes for lack of prey, and the sons of the lion are scattered.

6. Moreover a word stole upon me, and my ear caught a whisper of it; in distractions from visions of the night, when deep sleep falls upon mortals.

7. Dread cried out to me and trembling, and shook every bone of my body; a wind passed over my face, and the hair of my flesh bristled with horror.

8. It stood, and I did not turn from the sight of it. A form impalpable to my eyes. Silence, yet I heard a voice: SHALL MORTAL BE JUST BEFORE GOD? SHALL MAN SHINE MORE THAN HIS MAKER? Lo, He will not trust His servants, and imposes praise on His angels; much more those who dwell in houses of clay, whose foundation is in dust, who will be crushed before the moth.

9. Between morning and evening they will be shattered; from fear of the bystanders they will perish from glory.

5. *Fierce;* strictly *of the roarer, i.e.,* of a clamorous beast of prey.

6. *Moreover;* apparently Eliphaz descends here from the general to the particular, implying that the cause of Ayub's downfall had been intimated to him; and it seems quite possible that Satan had acted in the matter for the express purpose of assailing Ayub through Eliphaz.

Mortals; Gesenius does not connect the word with one differently pointed, meaning *to be sick, ill at ease;* but as pointing is a modern invention it seems hardly possible to bring forward reasons for the opinion.

8. *Imposes praise on his angels;* this seems to be the intention. According to the usual pointing the word translated *praise* only occurs here, and Gesenius, by an ingenious but not convincing course of reasoning, would render it *folly,* according to the usual rendering. Unpointed, however, the word is simply that translated *Psalm,* and stands in the plural unpointed at the head of each page of the PSALMS in the Hebrew.

9. *The bystanders;* Gesenius gives the meaning of the word as *attending.* The translation is perhaps not in accord with the pointing, but it seems impossible to make sense any other way.

Are not their cords undone? They will die, and that without any artifice being used against them.

10. Call now, if any will attend to you, and to which of the shrines will you turn? For as for the fool, anger will slay him; and jealousy will kill the simple.

11. I saw a fool flourishing and recognised his abode at once. Their sons will be far from deliverance, they will be crushed in the gate, and there will be none to rescue them. Whose harvest hunger will devour, and he will not save them from thorns, the snare pants for their strength.

12. For though ennui springs not from dust, and vexation sprouts not out of the ground; yet man is born to vexation, and the sons of flame fly aloft.

13. I will seek counsel at the Mighty, and before God

9. *Are not their cords undone? i.e.,* Are they not taken down like a tent?

Without any artifice being used against them; this seems to be the meaning, literally *not with dexterity, skill,* of an artificer. The intention is not that men are wicked, but that they are as devoid of personality as a tent and are used accordingly.

10. *Call now;* these words are the beginning of a new chapter in existing versions, and here evidently Eliphaz speaks again in his own person; that which precedes being the utterance which he heard in his dream.

Simple; the word means *to spread out, to open,* and intransitively *to be of open and ingenuous mind,* like children and young people. Eliphaz clearly indicates his opinion that his friend is suffering for his childlike simplicity of character; one would think he had taken out a brief for Satan to reduce him to despair.

11. *In the gate;* where trials were held and were men assembled for business or pleasure. *To be crushed in the gate* therefore means, to be worsted in the encounter with one's fellows in business, pleasure, or judgment.

12. *Ennui;* Gesenius says *emptiness, vanity,* but here the intention is clearly what we call *ennui, boredom.*

The sons of flame; apparently meaning the *Heaven-abiders.* Our English versions seem to miss the intention: LXX. paraphrases *The brood of the vulture.* Still if *sons of flame* be taken to mean sparks, we have a double sense, such as we constantly find in Scripture, the mistake is to accept the meaner and more fleshly sense as the true intention.

will I order my words. Magnificent are His works, and there is no searching out mysteries; eternity cannot be reckoned.

14. He gives rain upon the face of the earth, and sends forth waters upon the face of wildernesses; to place the lowly on high, and ragged ones rise to positions of influence.

15. From lots, from meditations, they go naked; and their hand performs not their counsel. He takes the skilful in their craft, and the contrivances of counsellors are rashness itself.

16. By day they rush upon darkness, and grope at noonday as if it were night. And He will preserve the needy from their sword, from their mouth, and from the hand of might. And there will be hope for the feeble, and iniquity closes her mouth.

17. Lo, the happiness of the man whom God disciplines, and who rejects not the correction of the Almighty. For

13. *I.* The personal pronoun is strongly emphasised both here and in the following clause, Eliphaz in fact counsels his friend to take a hint from himself.

Counsel; עוּלם is a word that seems to puzzle lexicographers, but seems very possibly an archaic form of the word علم = *science,* still current in the East. Some read אוּלם which does not seem an improvement.

At the Mighty; or perhaps *at God,* but he does not specify any one personally.

Eternity cannot be reckoned; or *Even past reckoning;* or *The witnesses there is no recording, i.e.,* they are numberless. All three seem possible renderings, and the point is the same whichever we take.

Positions of influence; the idea of the word is that of *ample space,* the converse of *straits.*

15. *Craft;* the usual rendering, but the root meaning is *nakedness.* Evidently the intention is that human skill and craft are mere nakedness, before the gods; which is perfectly true, but for the true moral, see Apoc. iii. 15—19.

16. *From their mouth;* compare Psalm LVII. 4, A.V.

17. Here as in many places the words of Eliphaz are above reproach, but his suggestions are hateful. Here for instance he appears to be counselling Ayub to submit—somewhat as his wife did before—but what form his submission is to take does not appear.

He will cause pain, and will bind up ; He will smite, and His hand will heal.

18.   In six distresses He will deliver you, and in seven evil shall not touch you.   In famine He will release you from death, and in war from the hand of the sword.

19.   When the scourge of the tongue is abroad you shall be hid, and shall not tremble at violence when it comes.   At violence and at envy you shall laugh, and shall not tremble at the life of the earth.

20.   For with the stones of the field shall you be in covenant, and the life of the field will be friendly to you ; and you feel that your tent is sound, and you shall reach your habitation and not miss it.

21.   And you shall know that your seed shall be abundant, and your harvest as grass on earth.   You shall come to your tomb in old age, like offerings heaped up seasonably.

22.   Lo, these things we have searched out.   So it is. Hear them, and frame your thoughts accordingly.

V.   AND AYUB REPLIED and said : Oh, that my wrongs were duly weighed, and my outcries lifted in the balances with them !   For now they are heavier than the sand of the sea, therefore my

19. *Envy;* the root meaning is *to pine,* from hunger or thirst, here evidently of envy.

Life of the earth ; the usual rendering is *beasts,* and no doubt it is animal life that is referred to.   But see the next words.

21. *Harvest ;* or *produce,* but evidently metaphorical of *offspring.*   Eliphaz says this shall be like grass, *i.e.,* for abundance, but he does not seem to reflect that grass though excellent in its place is hardly an ideal harvest.

22. *Frame your thoughts accordingly ;* this is hardly satisfactory as a translation, but the Hebrew is obscure.   That this is the general intent seems pretty certain.

language was bitter. For the arrow of violence has transfixed me, whose heat drinks my rest; the terrors of a god
are arrayed against me.

2. Does the wild ass neigh over fresh pasture, or
an ox low over dainty provender? Is insipidity swallowed
because it lacks savour, or is there taste in the filth of
dreams? My soul refuses to touch these, they are as
loathesome as my food.

3. Who will give me to attain my request? Oh that
God would grant me my hope, and God would consent and
crush me, that he would put forth his hand and finish me.
And I should have consolation again; I would leap and

1. *Wrongs;* or more exactly *provocations.* Ayub exclaims against the lack of
sympathy manifested by Eliphaz in rebuking his passion rather than in considering the provocations of which it is the outcome. LXX. have: " Oh, for
someone to justify my anger, and lift my pangs in the balances with it."
Bitter; Gesenius says *rash*, but does not support it in any way. Compare
the word for *wormwood*, which seems akin. See also Ruth i. 20.
The arrow of violence; the usual rendering *of the Almighty* seems not
to be justified by the word nor in harmony with the context. It was not the
arrow of the Almighty, but of Satan, the homicide; and Ayub seems quite
aware of it. How should mortal exist if shot down by the Almighty?
Similarly in the second clause. Ayub is not so mad as to suppose that he is
contending with Jehovah.
2. *In the filth of dreams.* This is bad as a translation, as it makes Ayub
say with brutal plainness what he appears to have avoided saying. Gesenius
is probably right in translating, *in the slime of purslain, i.e.,* in broth made of
a herb proverbial for insipidity. Yet the word is so like that for *dreams* that
the point could hardly be missed.
As my food. Ayub does not say his friend's words are despicable or
wrong in themselves, but merely that they are out of place in comparison
with the greatness of the wrongs which have befallen him and the pain he is
enduring. What could be further from Ayub's thought or wish than the
presumption apparently ascribed to him by Eliphaz in connection with the
dream he relates?
3. *Finish me;* or *break me off.* Gesenius seems right in saying the
metaphor is taken from the weaver's art when he breaks off the finished web.
Consolation. So Gesenius, but the connection with the root meaning is
not obvious; but the passage is difficult throughout.

B

dance and would not spare, for I would not disown holy words.

4. What is my strength that I should hope, and what is my end that I should prolong my life? Is my strength that of a pair of mill-stones? Is my flesh copper? Or have I any help that I should fear to thrust it from me?

5. When one faints his friends fall away, and the respect of the mighty forsakes him. My brethren have dealt treacherously like a brook; they have vanished like the bed of brooks which are turbid from ice when the snow has hidden itself in them. What time they dwindle they are silent, when it is hot they disappear from their place.

6. They turned aside the paths of their going, they went off into the desert and were lost. The paths of Tema beheld them, the ways of Saba expected them. They were ashamed that confidence had found entrance on the subject, and

3. *I would not disown holy words.* Apparently referring to his previous rejection of Eliphaz' words, but the Hebrew is obscure.

5. *From ice;* perhaps meaning from the result of an avalanche falling into the channel and blocking it until at last it is melted, and the water ponded up by it bursts through with a rush causing a fearful inundation below. The Caubul River at Naushera has run backwards before now owing to such an obstruction in the upper Indus. The stream being inordinately swollen the *bed* disappears altogether, and the traveller meets an unfordable torrent. On the other hand, in the heat of summer there will be no water at all. The point seems to be that they have no constancy, but are the mere creatures of circumstance.

6. *The paths;* this seems to be the meaning of the word, and why it should be rendered *troops* does not appear. Similarly the word rendered *ways* is made to mean *companies* or *caravans*, but no sufficient reason is given. In both cases the intention seems to be that his brethren have wandered off like wild Arabs of the desert when they should have brought him help and consolation. Tema means *desert*. For what the Sabæans were capable of, see i. 10, *ante*.

blushed. For now you had been his, you had seen terror and had trembled.

7. Or did I say, Give me? Or, Of your might bestow a gift in my behoof? Or, Rescue me from the hand of the enemy, and release me from the hand of the terrible?

8. Overawe me and I will be silent. What is my error? Demonstrate it to me. How powerful are right words! But what does your reproving establish? Do you think to argue down with words, and with the wind of discourse devoid of hope?

9. Moreover you overthrow the orphan, and dig the pit for your friend. And now be content. Turn to me, and to your face I ask if I lie? Turn, I pray you, let there be no distortion. And turn again, my uprightness is in it. Is there distortion in my tongue? Cannot my palate discern ——?*

10. Is there not a host for man upon earth, and his days like the days of a hireling? As a slave pants for shade,

6. *You had seen terror.* The meaning here seems to be that if his friends had dared to behave with Ayub's straightforwardness and simplicity or to approve of it in him they would have risked sharing his sufferings, and would have had more reason to tremble than Eliphaz found in his dream.

* Here occurs a word of which lexicographers seem able to give no account, but the sense seems tolerably complete without it. Ayub seems at this point to cease addressing Eliphaz directly, and in current translations a new chapter is commenced; but it seems better to avoid introducing the break so near the end of Ayub's speech.

10. *A host;* the word is the familiar *Sabaoth* in the singular, and the meaning *army, host,* seems pretty certain though perhaps the intention is given by translating *warfare.* The key seems to lie in the fact that Ayub really under-stood what St. Paul taught long after, that man is set to contend against spiritual foes; and that he Ayub was personally engaged in such a contest, and could not expect rest or comfort until the strife was over. Still it seems a hard thing that his brother man should side with his mortal foes—and their own—rather than seek to comfort and strengthen him.

and as a hireling for his work; so I am being made to inherit months of calamity, and nights of weariness are assigned to me.

11. Lo, I lie down and say, When shall I arise? And the evening stretches before me, and I am full of tossings till the dawn. My flesh is clothed with worms and dust, my skin trembles and melts; my days are swifter than a weaver's shuttle, and are spent without hope.

12. Remember that my life is a breath, my eye will not return to see good. No eye will turn to me, your eye looks upon me and sees nothing.

13. A cloud vanishes and is gone, so he who goes down to the grave will not return. He will not return to his house, neither shall his place know him any more.

14. Nay, I will not speak obscurely, I will talk according to the distress of my spirit, I will speak according to the bitterness of my soul.

15. Am I a sea, or a sea-monster, that you set watch

10. *For his work;* this is the simple meaning, and there seems to be no reason whatever to render it *hire.* Indeed, in A.V. *reward* is printed in italics, but there is no necessity to supply the word; compare Matt. xx. 6, 7.

The evening stretches before me; as a time of desperate tedium instead of one of rest and recreation. This seems to be the intention.

Trembles and melts; assigning to the words the meanings given by Gesenius, though he goes out of the way to assign them a different meaning here. Ayub seems to say it is useless to talk about how he came into such a plight, what he wants is present sympathy and help.

12. *Sees nothing;* or more exactly, *I am nothing, i.e.,* in your sight, apparently alluding to Eliphaz' speech, which shewed that he could not see or wilfully ignored the real issue, and could only reprove him with folly in adhering to simplicity and straight-dealing, when every one knows they do not pay. Ayub's case seemed to shew they did until Satan's jealousy was aroused.

14. *Speak obscurely;* or *be dark of mouth,* which seems to be the closest rendering. Ayub seems to say he is not going to pretend to be content in such utter misery, or to admit that he has consciously done aught to bring it on himself.

over me ? If I say my couch shall comfort me, my bed shall bear my discourse; you break me with dreams, and distract me with visions, and my soul because of stranglings prefers death to my bones.

16. I melted, but not from desire ; I shall be wanting from my lot, like Abel his days.

17. What is man, that Thou makest him great, and that Thou settest Thine heart upon him, and visitest him every morning, and triest him every ·moment ? How long wilt Thou regard my lot ? Thou wilt not let me alone while I swallow down my spittle.

18. Have I been wanting? What shall I do to Thee, Thou watcher of men? Why dost set me as a mark for Thee, so that I am a burden to myself? And why dost not lift my transgression and pass over my perversity? For now I should lie down in the dust, and Thou shouldst seek me and I should not be.

15. *Dreams.* Perhaps referring to Eliphaz' statement about the vision he had seen, and which he evidently meant had special reference to Ayub. The Scripture says death came by *man*, and we see every day how man is brought to grief by and through his brother man. *Homo homini lupus*, is an overtrue saying. When men learn care for each other, after the teaching of the *Son of man*, instead of adopting the suggestions of the manslayer, human nature will have a chance.

To my bones. The meaning is obscure, but perhaps Satan had not visited Eliphaz alone, but Ayub also with dreams, and in such fashion that his soul preferred death to association with his bones, which were made vehicles of torture to him. Compare Ps. xlii. 10, A.V.

16. *Like Abel;* the only way of making sense seems to take the word as a proper name, and to suppose that Ayub is reminding Eliphaz that he is in danger of enacting the part of Cain.

17. It is not at all clear who is addressed here, but apparently it is the Unseen Powers in general.

In this concluding part of the chapter Ayub seems to turn from his human companions to the Unseen whence, as he evidently recognises, his sufferings come. He appears to ask what it is possible for him to have done which could injure any of the Unseen Powers about him, and supposing he has displeased Them, why they do not finish him and end the matter.

VI. A ND BILDAD THE SHUHITE REPLIED and said : How long will you utter these things and the utterance of your mouth be a strong wind? Does a Strong one pervert judgment, or the Almighty twist justice?

2. Have your sons been wanting towards Him, and He cast them down by the hand of sinners Are YOU seeking to the strong, and respectful to the Almighty ? Are YOU pure and upright that now you should awake compassion over you, and an abode should be secured you as your right? Your descent is from nobody, and your end will wander far astray.

3. For ask now of the generation of the patriarchs, and check yourself by the investigation of the fathers ; for we are of yesterday and shall not know, for our days are a shadow upon earth. Shall not THEY teach you? They will tell you, and will utter words from their heart.

2. The suggestion seems, from what precedes, as well as what follows, to be that Ayub's children had not fallen by the hand of *sinners*, but by the just judgment of the Almighty. In fact Bildad is blind to the dealings of the Almighty, and seems to see no God but Satan the manslayer.

Compassion; this word is supplied, as the verb requires an object in English; though the Hebrew can dispense with it.

Your descent is from nobody; this seems to be the meaning. Ayub is not represented as of noble birth ; in fact nothing whatever is said of his parentage, and the point of the book seems to be precisely that God is no respecter of persons but rewards right conduct in humble and lofty alike.

Wander astray. This seems to be the only way of making sense, though it involves a change in the pointing. But after all the change is not great, for Gesenius describes it as pointed as an unused root, meaning *to be level, spread out,* which seems to suggest the end of many rivers in Central Asia, which never reach the sea but lose themselves in the desert sands.

3. Even in Ayub's day the book of Enoch was in existence, and he does not appear to have been the only antediluvian writer by any means. That his book should have been preserved through the Cataclysm presents no difficulty, for if Noah could read at all—and he was decidedly an educated and able man —he would be sure to save his library. How else would he while away the tedious months of imprisonment ?

4. Does the papyrus spring up except in a marsh, or the rush grow away from water? While it is yet in its greenness, will it not be cut off, and dry up from among the grass.

5. So are the ways of all who forget God, and the hope of the impious will perish. Whose strength is despicable; and their house—A spider is their confidence.

6. He will lean upon his house and it will not stand; he will bind it fast to him and it will not remain.

7. He is full of sap before the sun, and his suckers go forth over his garden. His roots twine themselves about the stone-heap, he sees the house of stones.

8. Will he swallow him down from his place? It will disown him, saying I have not seen you. Lo, this is the rejoicing of his road, and from dust in the end they will sprout forth.

9. Lo, God will not despise the whole-hearted, and will not bind him by the hand of evil-doers. Until he fill your mouth with laughter and your lips with shouting.

4. *From among;* literally *from the face of.* The intention evidently is that in the absence of excessive moisture such growths disappear at once, and it is not difficult to see that Bildad is in his mind comparing his friend to such a growth.

The fact is men are *impious* relatively, those who worship not the Cross are held impious by professing Christians, and those who bow not to the *Host* by the Roman Church.

7. Evidently Bildad has in his mind Ayub's transient prosperity and the way his sons kept open house and feasted in their time. Hospitality is counted a virtue among the Arabs and kindred nations, but doubtless their profusion was regarded as extravagant and presumptuous.

8. This is obscure, but is probably an allusion to the way trees in the mountains often seem to grow without much earth, clinging on to the almost bare rock and thrusting their roots into the crevices.

Such a tree if blown down by the wind leaves no hole, and it seems incredible that it should have grown where it did.

9. *Whole-hearted;* the intention of the word seems to be *Upright,* straightforward and simple in conduct.

10. Those that hate you will be clothed with shame, and the tent of the wicked is naught.

VII.   AND AYUB REPLIED and said: In truth I know that it is so; and shall man be just with God? If He stoop to plead with him he cannot answer one in a thousand. Wise is His heart and firm His strength; who has been stubborn with Him and continued safe?

2. Who overturns mountains, and they perceive not how He has turned them in His anger. Who shakes the earth from her place, and her pillars are broken.

3. Who speaks to the sun and it rises not, and seals up the stars. Who stretches out the heavens alone, and treads upon the heights of the sea.

4. He made the Wain, Orion, and the Pleiades; and

---

10. Bildad seems to exhort Ayub to humble himself before it is too late, and to lay aside his presumption, so that he may not be found among those previously described.

2. *Mountains;* the prophetic symbol of kingdoms, and sometimes apparently of kings and rulers.

Her pillars are broken. Perhaps referring to the catastrophe of the Cataclysm, then fresh in men's minds, to appreciate which it is necessary to read the book of Enoch and the account of Moses with intelligence.

3. Here again we probably have an echo of Noah's experience in the ark.

Alone; seems to mean here *unaided.* The simile is that of pitching a tent, and even a small tent can hardly be pitched by a single man.

Heights; Gesenius would render it *fortresses,* by analogy with Amos iv. 13, where A.V. and R.V. have *high-places* of the earth.

This seems intelligible enough, a fortress being commonly built on an inaccessible peak, if possible; but it is probable that the *sea* spoken of is the ocean of ether in which the earth is afloat. It may be well to remind the reader that in Greek, ἀνάγειν ναῦν means *to put out to sea,* κατάγειν ναῦν, to bring to land. And in English *the high seas* means the open ocean.

4. *Pleiades;* or the *Cluster,* which Gesenius seems to identify without much room for doubt. The other constellations he shews less reason for

the chambers of the South. He does great things until there is no searching them out, and marvels till there is no telling them.

5. Lo, He passes over me and I see Him not, He laughs and I perceive not what He is doing. Lo, He seizes and who shall turn Him aside? Who will say to Him, What wilt do?

6. If a god turn not aside his wrath, beneath him the proud helpers are humbled. How much less should I answer him, or attempt words with him. Whom if I were upright I would not answer, I would come to terms with my opponent.

7. If I called and he answered me I would not believe that he heard my cry; seeing he gapes upon me with terrors, and multiplies my wounds without cause. He will not allow me to draw my breath, for he will fill me with bitterness.

8. If I speak of strength! Lo, a Strong One: If for judgment! Who will appoint me a hearing? If I have a

identifying thus, but he is probably correct. They are the most conspicuous constellations in the Northern Heavens. It is noteworthy that he states that the *Bear* as the name of a constellation seems to be a perversion; it should rather be *Bier*, from the verb bear, not the noun—*i.e.*, in the science of the Orientals.

5. *Seises;* Gesenius gives the meaning *to seise, ravin,* as a lion, *i.e.,* to pounce upon his prey.

6. *Answer.* It should be remembered that the catastrophe of the book is precisely that the Almighty will not leave Ayub until he answers him and learns to converse with him.

Opponent; or *adversary,* in the language of A.V., meaning an *opponent at law.* Compare Matt. v. 25.

7. Ayub does not say who he is speaking of, but the book shews that it was not the Almighty but the godling Satan who was tormenting him. Still, of course, he could do nothing but what he was permitted to do, and herein lay Ayub's real confidence.

just cause my mouth will condemn me; I am heart-whole but it will undo me.

9. I perfect! I do not see my breath, I despise my life. It were all one as if I said, Integrity and wickedness have here attained perfection.

10. If the scourge slay suddenly he will laugh at the trial of the innocent victims. The earth is given into the hand of the wicked, the face of her judges he covers. If not, who is this?

11. My days are swifter than a runner; they fleet by, they see no good. They glide away like vessels of reed; as an eagle swoops upon its prey.

12. If I say I will forget my tale; I will relax my face and be cheerful: I fear all my pains, I see that thou wilt not acquit me. If I am guilty, why do I draw this painful breath?

13. If I wash myself with snow-water, and make my hands clean at the spring; thereupon thou wilt plunge me in the ditch, and my clothes will abhor me.

14. For he is not a man like me; shall I answer Him? Shall we go in together for judgment? There is not an arbitrator between us to lay his hands upon us both.

15. He will remove his rod from off me, and His firmness

---

10. Apparently the thought is that man is altogether at so imperfect a stage of existence that his sufferings are no more heeded than those of blind kittens that are drowned; and perhaps that the very destruction is really an advance in the scale of existence.

If not, who is this? Ayub apparently means, How or Why or Whence have his overwhelming misfortunes come.

11. *Vessels of reed;* probably because of their temporary nature and frail material rather than any particular swiftness. Boats of papyrus were used on the Nile, but they could hardly be anything but temporary make-shifts; a permanent craft would be built of stronger material.

13. See Shakespeare's Tempest, Act iv., latter part of the scene.

will not terrify me. I will speak and will not fear Him, for not so am I with myself.

16. My soul loathes my life ; I will let loose upon me my discourse, I will speak according to the bitterness of my soul.

17. I will say to God, Thou wilt not declare me guilty! Shew me over what Thou wilt strive with me. Is it good in Thy sight to oppress, to despise the work of Thy hands, and to shine upon the counsel of the wicked ?

18. Hast Thou eyes of flesh? Shalt Thou see as man sees? Are Thy days as the days of a man, or Thy Years as the days of a hero? That Thou wilt seek to ruin me, and wilt track my faults ?

19. Thou knowest that I am not guilty, and there is none to pluck me out of Thy hand. Thy hand fashioned me and wrought me alone on all sides, and wilt Thou eat me up ?

20. Remember, I pray Thee, that Thou didst fashion me of clay, and wilt turn me to dust again. Hast Thou not poured me out like milk and curdled me as it were into cheese ?

21. Skin and flesh Thou hast made my clothing, and hast fenced me with bones and muscles. With life and love Thou didst endow me, and Thy care guarded my spirit.

22. And these things Thou hast hidden in Thine heart, I know that this is with Thee.

23. Have I been wanting? But Thou didst watch over me, and wilt Thou not cleanse me from my perversity?

24. Have I been wicked? WOE is me. Or righteous? I will not lift up my head. I am full of shame, and see my

---

19. Compare ii. 2, *ante*. " And you incited Me against him *to eat him up*." The Hebrew word is the same in both places.

22. *With Thee; i.e., chez toi.* The meaning seems to be that these are acts of the Almighty of which He cannot but be cognisant.

affliction; and if it should raise itself, like a lion Thou wilt hunt me, and wilt turn and distinguish Thyself upon me.

23. Thou wilt renew Thy witness against me and multiply provocations upon me. A succession of hosts is against me, and why didst bring me forth from the womb?

26. I shall expire and eye shall see me no more; for as if I had no existence I shall be, from the womb to the grave I shall be carried.

27. Are not my days few? Cease then; put away from me and mine, and I will be cheerful a little; before I go whence I shall not return.

28. To a land of darkness and shadows; a land of darkness like the depth of shadows, and without order; whose very radiance is obscurity.

VIII. AND ZOPHAR THE NAAMATHITE replied and said: Should not the multiplication of words be repressed, and shall a man of lips be right? Your foolish talk stuns men, you babble and there is no putting you to shame.

2. And you say, I have been purely passive, and I am

---

22. *If it should raise itself;* apparently meaning his head. *Like a lion; as if I were a lion.* At least this seems to be the intention. Ayub apparently is afraid of suffering the fate which Pharaoh afterwards incurred, in case he hardens his heart. See Rom. ix. 14-18.

23. *A succession of hosts;* this certainly seems to be the intention. Gesenius renders it "Changes and hosts are against me," and so explains the intention. The word rendered *changes* is especially used of soldiers relieving guard.

26. *I shall be carried;* there is a certain emphasis on the personal pronoun. Ayub says his lot seems to be that of pure passivity, and he is carried through this mortal life like a corpse, on a bier. Compare (in original) Lc. xxiv. 46, noting that πάσχω means *to receive an impression* from without, as opposed to *doing* any thing.

2. *I have been purely passive;* this seems to be the intention. The Hebrew is very succinct, *My taking is pure,* i.e., unmixed, untainted; which may have

clear in Thine eyes. Whereas who ever gave a word to God? And will He open His lips to talk with you? And will He show you secrets of science and skill? For wisdom is manifold, and know that God has remitted for you part of your guilt.

3. Will you search out the depths of God? Will you investigate the perfection of the Almighty? Heaven is high! What will you do? Hell is deep! What is your rage? Measures longer than the earth and broader than the sea.

4. Will He glide by, shut up, call together? Who will turn Him aside? For He knows that men are unreliable, and sees their emptiness and will not attend. For man is void of heart, and the sons of Adam like the wild ass's colt.

5. Will you set up your heart, and spread out your hands to Him? Is vanity in your hand? Put it away and it will not cause the wicked to dwell in your tent. For

several meanings, *e.g.*, " My way of taking things is simple and plain," and so not open to blame. The usual rendering, " My doctrine is pure," seems very wide of the mark, as Ayub has made no endeavour to teach any one, and his attitude suggests the words, " Si rixa est ubi tu pulsas ego vapulo tantum."

2. *Wisdom is manifold;* Gesenius renders it " God's wisdom has double folds." Compare Eph. iii. 10. Rather it would seem to mean " The constitution of the universe is complex," but since the universe is the expression of the Creator this seems to be nearly the same thing in different words.

Has remitted; Hebraicé *caused to forget.*

3. *Rage;* Under this word Gesenius gives: " *To be evil* (properly, *to rage, to make a noise, to be tumultuous*)."

4. Gesenius has a long note on this passage, which does not seem to need much explanation. The point for English readers to note seems to be that the *heart* in Hebrew, as in Greek, often means the seat of feeling and sense whereby we become conscious of impressions from without and interpret the indications of the senses. So in English *heartless* conduct means such as is devoid of consideration for others. Compare Mc. vi. 51, 52; vii. 18–23; viii. 17–21.

5. *Cause the wicked to dwell in your tent.* This seems to be another way of saying, it will not make you a wicked man.

then you will lift up your face from blame, and you have been poured out and will not tremble.

6. For YOU will forget afflictions, and as waters passed away will you remember them; and your time will arise brighter than noonday, you shall fly and be as the morning. And you trusted that there is hope: you were ashamed? You shall lie down in security.

7. And you lay down and there was none who disturbed, and multitudes stroked your face. And the eyes of the wicked shall waste away, and refuge shall be lost to them, and their hope is the breathing out of life.

IX. AND AYUB REPLIED and said: I know that you are the people, and with you science shall die. Still I have sense even as you, I have not fallen worse than you. Indeed who is wanting in matters like these?

2. I am become the laughing-stock of my neighbours, one that called on God—and He answered him! Scorn is

5. *Poured out;* like molten metal seems to be the intention, but see verse 20 of the last chapter. The usual rendering *stedfast* seems only capable of justification in a round-about fashion, as we might say, you have been *cast-iron;* but the simpler way is rather, "You have been molten and run like metal and did not blench, and need fear nothing in the future."

7. *The breathing out of life;* i.e., *expiration, death.*

1. *That you are the people;* that is according to Gesenius the whole human race—evidently much in the vein in which Carlyle said, "The population of Great Britain is —— millions, mostly fools."

Science; or *wisdom* of a practical kind, in fact the science of life.

Sense; Hebraicé *heart,* see previous note.

righteous and just. A torch despised in the opinion of the careless, a foot prepared for the assembly.

3. The tents of the violent are secure, and confidence is for those who provoke God, to whom God gives abundantly in their hand.

4. But indeed ask now the dumb animals and they will instruct you, and the birds of heaven and they will tell you; or talk to the earth and it will teach you, and the fish of the sea will tell you.

5. Who has not trembled at all these? For the hand of Jehovah fashioned these things, inasmuch as by His hand all life had breath, and all flesh of man spirit. Does not the ear try discourse, and the palate taste a man's food?

6. With grey hairs wisdom, and with length of days understanding! With Him is wisdom, and He has strength, resource, and backbone.

7. Lo, He will destroy and there is no building up, He will shut down and there is no opening. Lo, He will shut up the sea and it will dry up, and He will send and turn the earth upside down.

2. *Scorn is righteous and just.* This seems to be the intention, viz., that his neighbours regard him as justly laughed at for supposing that God would pay any attention, and think by so doing to justify God—and so they do justify the god of this world, but he is Satan the man-slayer.

A *foot prepared for the assembly;* what this may mean is difficult to see, but it seems to be the translation of the words. Perhaps the intention is that it is only for a single occasion, after which it is to be thrown aside as done with.

4. Verily, verily, I say to you, unless any one has been born of water and wind he cannot enter into the Reign of God. Jno. iii. 5. See also Matt. vi. 26—34.

5. Compare " What are the wild waves saying."

7. *Shut up.* Compare (in original) Mc. iv. 39-41. The Greek word which A.V. renders " Peace " is literally *Be mussled;* that is Hold your tongue, shut up.

Turn the earth upside down. Compare Acts xvii. 6, A.V.

8.　With Him is Might and He has Counsel. Sinner and perverter are His. He makes counsellors go naked ; and judges he will expose.

9.　He loosens the bonds of kings, and will bind the girdle upon their loins. Causing priests to go naked, and overturning the stable. Removing the lip of the trusty, and taking captive the discernment of elders. Pouring contempt on princes, and loosening the girdles of officials.

10.　Unveiling depths hidden in darkness, and dragging to light the shadow of death. Multiplying the nations and destroying them, spreading out the nations and leading them forth.

11.　Depriving of sense the heads of the people of the earth, He will cause them to wander in a trackless waste ; they will grope in the dark and have no light, and He will make them wander as if drunk.

---

8. It seems to be practically forgotten that to *judge* another is inconsistent with the merest elements of the doctrines of Christ, see how St. Paul insists upon this, Rom. ii. 1, 21-24. Also how cunningly he avoids the position himself, 1 Cor. v. 12, 13. A passage by the way which the A.V. perverts into an injunction to practise the very vice St. Paul is teaching them to avoid. It should be : *Therefore curse the devil out of yourselves.* Not " Put away that wicked person."

9. *Of the trusty ;* So the Jewish School and Family Bible. Gesenius gives *tried, approved,* counsellors. Compare II. Sam. xv. 31.

Officials ; the word strictly means *a channel, tube,* and is clearly used here of *subordinates* who act as channels for the action of a prince.

10. *Leading them forth.* Gesenius would render it leading them *back,* contrary to his own account of the meaning of the word and to the experience of mankind ; for nations who have once migrated seldom return, although individuals do. The words that follow look like a prophecy of the Exodus of Israel.

11. *As if drunk.* The point of this remark and of many others made by Ayub seems to be commonly missed, which is apparently this: That the Almighty does what He wills, and not only individuals but nations are helpless in His hand ; consequently those suffering chastisement at His hand are to be helped and supported, and not to be reproached as wicked by their fellow men. Compare Rom. xv. 1, remembering that though St. Paul speaks there in the first person,

12. Lo, my eye has seen it all, my ear has heard and understood it. As you know it, so do I also know it; I am not more fallen than you. But YOU are patching lies and sewing emptiness, the lot of you. Who will give a gag, that you might be silent; and it would be wisdom to you.

13. Hear now my arguments, and attend to the myriads of my words. Will you assign perversity to God, or attribute remissness to Him?

14. Will you shew Him countenance? Will you contend with the Almighty? Is it good that He should search YOU out? Will you mock Him as one mocks a man?

15. Assuredly he will rebuke YOU! Will you shew countenance in secret? Shall not His Majesty put you in fear, and His terror fall upon you? Your reminders are

he none the less penned such passages as I. Cor. iv. 8-13, xv. 32, II. Cor. vi. 3-10, vii. 5, xi. 24-21. See also James v. 7-11.

12. *I am no more fallen than you;* this seems to be the intention, Ayub says he is no doubt fallen, but not worse than his friends. They no doubt thought he ought to appear overwhelmed by his misfortunes; they should have known that the misfortune of one is the misfortune of all, and have been dismayed themselves at the extent of Ayub's calamities, fearing lest the like should befall them, seeing that no reason could be assigned for them. They should have been anxious to arrive at a solution of the problem, the meaning of the visitation; and whether others could avoid such, and if not what was the right course to pursue when so sorely smitten. So only could they be in sympathy with him or offer him comfort.

13. Ayub apparently means that whatever men suffer they must beware of reproaching the Almighty, and not for instance impute it to Him if man is such a feeble creature. He made man upright, and if he is weak and suffering it is deservedly so through his own folly; and the right course is to seek patiently where mistake has crept in, or how our heavenly Father has been offended if so it be.

15. The exact intention is obscure, but Ayub seems to fear lest his friends should *patronise* God, and says He will assuredly read their hearts if they do so, and act accordingly. See what He says to them at the end of the book.

maxims of ashes, your fortresses fortresses of clay. Be silent before me and I will speak myself, and what shall befall me ?

16. Over what have I lifted my flesh in my teeth, and taken my life in my hand ? Lo, He shall slay me, I did not hesitate ; only I will vindicate my way before Him. Moreover, I have this ground of confidence, that impiety shall not be imputed to His sons.

17. Listen, and hear my real meaning, and catch the breathings of my spirit in your ears. Lo now I have arranged the matter for trial, I know that I have a sound case.

18. Who is this? Will he contend against me that I am to be silent at the crisis, I who am dead.

15. *Fortresses of clay ;* so Gesenius renders it, which seems as good as anything for the intelligent reader, although earthworks are not despicable things in modern warfare.

Ayub seems to say that rather than listen to them he must speak himself, though averse to talk if it could be avoided. In fact he sees that to hold his peace and be classed with them is a greater danger than he can incur by repudiating their words.

16. *Hesitate ;* strictly to *remain, delay ;* often rendered *expect, hope,* but the simpler meaning seems more appropriate here.

His sons. The Church of England teaches her children that they are "members of Christ, children of God, and inheritors of the kingdom of heaven."

17. *Real meaning ;* properly *fulness, i.e.,* πλήρωμα, *that which fills.* Ayub begs them to dive into the ocean below, and leave off talking about mere surface effects. What follows is certainly somewhat amplified, but it is often impossible to imitate the brevity of the Hebrew without losing the sense in English.

18. *Who is this ?* Ayub's contention seems to be that he does not complain of the Almighty, Who has never afflicted him, but wants to come to an issue with his unseen persecutor and know how he has offended him, and if he appeals to the Almighty it is in order to get his case heard, and his fault, if there is any, explained to him. How many act as if it were so ?

I who am dead ; or, perhaps, *Why I should die on the spot.* Ayub seems to have, so far, at least, discerned between the Almighty and the godling Satan as to feel that any paltering with the latter would be fatal to him.

19. Only two things do not against me, then I shall not be hidden from thy presence: Remove thy hand from off me; and thy terror shall not overwhelm me. But call and I will reply, or I will speak and do Thou restore me.

20. For what are my crimes and shortcomings? Shew me my transgression and my failure. Why wilt Thou turn away Thy face and count me as Thine enemy? Wilt shake a leaf driven by the wind, and hunt a dry straw?

21. For Thou writest bitter things against me, and makest me inherit the sins of my youth. And Thou settest my feet in the stocks, and watchest all my ways; and Thou underminest the soles of my feet. And this will fall away like rottenness, like garments eaten by moth.

22. Man that is born of woman is brief of days and full of instability. Like a flower he springs up and is cut off; and he passes away like a shadow, and will not abide.

23. And on such a thing as this didst Thou open Thine eyes, and wilt Thou cause him to enter into judgment with Thee? Who ever brought a clean thing out of an unclean? Not one.

24. Are his days determined by the calculation of his months with Thee? Hast Thou made out his allotment

19. The intention here is obscure, but it would seem that Ayub's two requests are: 1st. That Jehovah should not forsake him altogether with his life in ruins; 2nd. That He will deal gently with him so that he may not be crushed by His might. He seems to contend that whatever he has done or left undone he has not been wantonly perverse, and therefore it is alien from the character of the Almighty to destroy him; compare Gen. xviii. 25.

22. *Born of woman;* that which is born of flesh is flesh. *Instability;* or more exactly, *trepidation* whether from fear, anger, or any other emotion.

24. *By the calculation of his months;* or more strictly by the *writing,* but the word is frequent both of computation and record. The meaning seems to be, Are his days given him as astrologers compute a horoscope; whereas the Almighty deals with men as they deal. With what measure ye mete it shall be measured to you again. Matt. vii. 2, A.V.

which he shall not pass? Look away from him and testimony will cease, his day will be paid off like a hireling.

25. For there is hope for a tree, if it shall be cut down and again spring up, that its suckers will not fail ; though its root grow old in the earth, and the trunk perish in the dust; at the scent of water it will burst forth and yield fruit as a plantation.

26. While man will die and fall prostrate, and Adam will expire and he is not. Waters rolled away from the midst of waters, and the stream dwindled and dried up; and man has lain down and will not get up; till the heavens fall they will not be sickened and awakened from their lethargy.

27. Oh, that Thou wouldst hide me in Sheol, that Thou wouldst cover me till Thy Spirit returns, that Thou wouldst appoint me a time and remember me then ! Shall man die ? Shall he live ? All the days of my service I wait till I am relieved.

24. *Testimony will cease;* apparently meaning that no notice will be taken.

25. The sense here seems to be missed in current renderings. Ayub says you may fell a tree, and the felled trunk may perish in the dust, yet the tree is not destroyed. Only give water and suckers will spring from the root, and from the decaying stem,and where there was one tree you will have a plantation.

26. *Man will die* . . . . This seems intelligible only by comparison of the lot of Adam with that of Enoch, the only exponent to Ayub of man's true hope and destiny.

Waters rolled . . . . Evidently to be understood by reference to many Central Asian rivers which never reach the sea but lose themselves in the deserts.

Will not be sickened . . . . Even the cataclysm failed to produce a lasting impression on the race. Sinai and Calvary are memories few attempt to understand. The wakening of individuals, as in Lear and Hamlet, to the worthlessness of this mortal life, is a fruitful subject with poets.

27. *Spirit;* this seems to be the intention, though some might render it countenance; the word is often used of the nose as the *breathing place,* but sometimes of pride, anger, &c., as shewn by hard breathing.

Days of my service . . . . Ayub evidently compares himself to a soldier on duty here, and says, he bides out his watch, however tedious, until the sentries are changed.

28. Thou wilt call, and how gladly will I answer Thee. Thou wilt long for the work of Thy hand.

29. Whereas now Thou wilt count my steps, and wilt not pass over my failings. My transgressions are collected in a file, and Thou patchest on to my perversity. But a mountain fallen lies prostrate, and will a stone move from its place?

30. Waters wear away stones; Thou sweepest away like a flood the dust of the earth, and the hope of man Thou destroyest. Thou wilt overpower him altogether, and his face will disappear from the year, and Thou wilt send him away.

31. His sons will become great and he sees it not, they will be despised, and he will not distinguish between them; only his flesh upon him will be distressed, and his breath upon him will fail.

X.

AND ELIPHAZ THE TEMANITE replied and said : Will a wise man's reply be knowledge of wind, and will he fill his belly with the East wind? Will he argue with words there is no understanding, and with unprofitable discourse?

28. Compare Isaiah xlix. 25.

29. *Collected in a file;* the Jewish School and Family Bible has *sealed up in a bundle,* evidently after the fashion of the French *dossier,* or the bundles tied with red tape common in English offices.

31. *Only his flesh.* The intention seems to be: " He has nothing but his flesh, which is heir to many ills; and his breath, which may fail at any moment."

1. *Knowledge of wind ;* the wisdom of God is foolishness with men and *vice versâ.* "Except a man be born of water and wind . . . ." See note under ix. 4, *ante.* One great point of the book seems to be the impossibility of any real understanding between Ayub and his three friends, due to the fact that they would not credit him with any deeper insight than they had themselves, or even with as much.

Unprofitable discourse. Perhaps *platitudes* would be better as expressing Eliphaz' meaning.

2. Moreover, YOU cast reverence to the winds, and restrain meditation before God ; for your mouth will teach your perversity, and your tongue selects nakednesses. Your mouth will condemn you and not I, and your lips will confute you.

3. Are you the first man that has been born, and were you begotten before the hills ? Will you be a listener at the council of God, and will you monopolise wisdom ?

4. What have you seen, and we shall not see it; or discerned that is not with us ? Moreover grey heads, more-over hoary eld, are with us, much older than your father.

5. Are the consolations of God slight in your estimation ? And a word involved to you ? What will take your heart, and at what will your gaze blench? For you will send back your breath to God, and spout forth words from your mouth.

6. What mortal man shall be clean, and shall one born of woman be righteous? Lo, He will not trust His saints, and the heavens are not clean in His eyes; much more detested and reprobate man, who drinks iniquity like water.

7. I will declare to you, hear me. This I have seen and I will set it forth. Which wise men have demonstrated, and they were not ignored by the fathers; to whom for their

---

2. The exact intention here is obscure, but Eliphaz seems shocked at his friend's outspokenness ; as most people are who have shirked trial, in the presence of those who have faced it.

5. *Gaze blench;* this seems to be the meaning. Gesenius gives the mean-ing to wink with the eyes, *as done in insolence or pride ! ! !* (the italics and notes of exclamation are mine). But the eyes wink simply for their own protection, the action is not one of insolence or pride.

portion was given the earth, and no stranger passed across in their midst.

8. All his days the unrighteous here is whirled about, and number of years is hidden from the headstrong. The voice of terrors is in his ears, in the midst of safety the oppressor will come upon him.

9. He will not hope to return from the midst of the dark; and his watchman, this for him is the sword. He wanders for food saying Where? He knows that a day of darkness is established in his hand.

10. An enemy shall come suddenly upon him, and distress shall overpower him like a king prepared for revolt. For he stretches out his hand even to God, and is contumacious towards the Almighty.

11. He will run upon him, upon his neck, upon his stoutness; shields his covering. For he has hidden his face in fatness, and he will prepare fat over his loins.

---

7. Here peeps out the cloven foot. Eliphaz ignores the fall and talks as if the earth had been given to man in his present condition; the fact being that at the fall man lost his position as king of the earth, and that he and it fell into the power of the manslayer. And as for no stranger finding an entrance among them. Why, the book of Enoch, the bible of that day, was the story of the intrusion of outsiders and the consequent corruption resulting in the Cataclysm.

8. *Headstrong;* this seems to be the sense, Gesenius gives *terrifying, fierce.* Eliphaz finds Ayub intractable, and therefore condemns him as contumacious. Compare what he said at first, iv. 5, *ante.*

10. *Revolt;* apparently meaning like a capable king who prepares beforehand for a popular rising, which he sees imminent. Gesenius' account of the word does not favour the usual rendering. Eliphaz says the unseen powers are on their guard against people like Ayub, and take care to be ready for them.

11. *Shields his covering;* apparently meaning protected with armour there is no hope of piercing.

Hidden in fatness; apparently equivalent to *veiled in indifference, stupidity.*

12. And he will dwell in hidden fortresses, houses that will not remain his, which are swift to become ruins. He will not prosper and his strength will not endure, and he shall not spread abroad upon the earth their wealth.

13. He will not get out of darkness, his sucker flame shall dry up, and he shall pass away with the breath of his mouth.

14. Let not the betrayed trust in destructiveness, for destruction shall be its own recompense. It shall not fulfil its days, and its branch shall not be green. It shall be as a vine that shakes off its grapes before they are ripe, and as an olive that casts its bloom.

15. For the assembly of the impious is barren, and fire devours the tent of open-handedness. He conceived toil and brought forth emptiness, and their womb will fashion deception.

XI. AND AYUB replied and said: I have heard myriads of such things as these; wearisome comforters are you all. Shall there be an end to words of spirit, or what will arouse you to respond?

2. Shall I talk to Him in your fashion? Do your words

---

12. *Wealth;* the word is a doubtful one and one manuscript reads *flocks,* which as far as Ayub was concerned would be much the same thing.

14. Apparently a heartless allusion to Ayub's bereaved condition.

15. *Fashion deception;* i.e., it will disappoint the hope it has aroused.

1. *Spirit;* translation here is very difficult for the word of course may be rendered *wind* just as legitimately. Ayub's words were spiritual and he knew it, while those of his would be comforters were mere wind in the sense they meant them.

go deeper than mine? I could weave words against you; and I could shake my head over you. I could make strong my mouth towards you, and make dark the consolation of my lips. If I speak I will not hide my pain; and if I abstain what will result?

3. Only now he has wearied me. Thou hast made desolate my whole assembly, and thou holdest me fast—it is clearly testified. And he has raised as it were my leanness before my face. It shall reply.

4. His anger has plucked me off, and he will set snares for me, he gnashed over me; in his teeth is my carcase, he will make sharp his eyes against me.

5. They gaped over me with their mouth, with scorn they smote against my life, with one consent they assembled against me. God will shut me up to evil, and He has cast me into the hand of wicked ones.

6. I was living securely and he broke me in pieces; he seized upon my neck and dashed me down, and set me up as a mark for himself.

7. They will turn upon me his hosts, he will cleave my very reins and will not spare, he will pour out my gall

2. *Deeper than mine;* the simple rendering seems to be, *Is your breath beneath mine?* apparently meaning does it penetrate deeper into the heart of the matter.

Make dark the consolation of the lips; i.e., speak words that wound and hurt instead of consoling.

4. *Carcase;* the dictionary meaning is *bundle,* and if we understand a bundle of papers to be meant, *i.e.,* the official record so to say of Ayub's case (an idea by no means foreign to some parts of the book of Enoch), we shall have instead of the above the picture of an angry official gnashing his teeth over a case he can find nothing in to justify his malice.

5. Compare what St. Paul says about fighting wild beasts at Ephesus.

6. *Mark;* apparently meaning a target to be shot at.

upon the earth. He will break me with breach upon breach, he will run upon me like a warrior.

8. I have sewn sack-cloth upon me as my skin, and sated my horn with dust. My face burns with weeping, and upon my eyelids is the shadow of death.

9. Moreover, there is no violence in my hand, and my prayer is clean. Oh, Earth ! Thou shalt not cover my blood, and there shall be no resting-place for my outcry.

10. Moreover, now lo, in the heavens is my witness, and in the heights I have an eye witness, an interpreter for me, a friend; my eye sheds tears to God.

11. And he will vindicate the stranger before God, the son of man to his friend. For the numbered years will come, and I go the way I shall not return.

12. My spirit is tortured and distressed, my days are extinguished, graves await me. Have not mockings waited upon me? And my eye dwells upon their maliciousnesses.

13. Order matters now, be my surety before Thee. Who is this that will strike hands with me? For Thou didst hide their hearts from seeing, Thou wilt not exalt them to honour. He betrays his friends to plunder, the eyes of his sons shall waste away.

14. And he will set me for a byword to the nations,

---

7. *Warrior;* or perhaps *athlete*, but the word evidently implies hostility as well as impetuosity and vigour.

8. *Sated ;* this seems best. Dust of course would be most repulsive and humiliating to the prosperous, but in his extremity Ayub seems to say it is positively welcome.

9. *Clean ;* probably here in the sense of *sincere, unfeigned*, free, that is from the taint of hypocrisy.

I shall be an object of loathing to them. My eye will fail from vexation, and all my frame is like a shadow.

15. The upright will be dumbfoundered over this, and the pure will rouse himself against the impious. And the righteous will grasp his road, and the man of clean hands will redouble his vigour, whereas all you shall be put to flight.

16. And come to the point now, and I shall not find a wise man among you. My days have passed by, my counsels have been torn to shreds, the wealth of my heart.

17. They will put night for day, light hard in front of darkness. Shall I wait? Sheol is my house; I have spread my bed in the dark. To the grave I called, Thou art my father; and to the worm, Thou art my mother and my sister.

18. Where now is my hope? And who will find hope for me? My limbs will go down into Sheol, lo they will go down together to dust.

XII. AND BILDAD THE SHUHITE replied and said: How long before you assign a limit to talk? You shall understand, afterwards we will speak.

2. What is the gain? Shall we be accounted as cattle? Have we polluted ourselves in your eyes? He tore his soul in his anger.

14. *Loathing;* properly *spittle,* meaning they would spit at the thought of him and his condition.

17. *Light hard in front of darkness.* Ayub seems to mean that light had shone upon him, only to be eclipsed at once.

1. *You shall understand;* this seems to be the meaning, though it is not clear who they are that shall understand.

3. On your account shall the bonds of the earth be loosed, and the rock be removed from its place?

4. Moreover the light of the wicked shall be extinguished, and the flame of his fire shall not shine. Light becomes darkness in his tent, and his lamp over him shall be put out.

5. The steps of his strength shall be straitened, and his counsel shall cast him down. For he is sent into a snare by his own feet, and he will walk himself into a net.

6. The noose shall seize upon his heel, and gins shall seize him fast. Nooses are hidden for him in the earth, and traps are piled upon him.

7. Calamities attack him on all sides and scatter him from his feet. His strength shall be hunger, and the burden is prepared for his ribs. It shall eat the portion of his skin; the first-born of death shall eat his portion.

8. He shall be torn away from his tent, and it will cause him to ascend to the King of Terrors. Thou wilt cause strangers to dwell in his tent; pitch shall be spread over his abode.

3. It looks as if Bildad were arguing that Ayub could not expect miracles to be wrought on his sole account.

4. Apparently yet another heartless allusion to the untimely end of Ayub's children. Bildad seems to be of the usual opinion that anyone who is suffering must have deserved it, an attitude which Christians at any rate should know would lead logically to the condemnation of their Lord Himself.

6. *Piled;* this is conjectural, but seems quite as probable as anything else. Gesenius connects the word with *to be lofty, swollen.*

7. *Calamities;* Gesenius says *terrors,* but the root meaning is rather this, which is supported in other ways.

For his ribs; apparently meaning that he will be treated as a mere beast of burden.

This is the usual rendering, the *first-born of death* being understood of the terrible disease from which Ayub was suffering. Certainly this seems to match the rest of the speech.

9. His roots below shall dry up, and above his foliage shall be cut off. His memory perished from the earth, and he shall have no name abroad.

10. They will thrust him from light into darkness, and thrust him from the world of men. There is no offspring from him, and no descendants about him, and no survivor of his pilgrimage.

11. His last traces fade with his day, and the ancients are stricken with terror. Only such are the dwellings of the wicked, and this is the abode of him who knows not God.

XIII.
AND AYUB replied. And he said : How long will you vex my soul, and crush me with your talk? This is ten times you have stabbed me! Are you not ashamed to stun me thus? And admitting I went astray, my error remains with me.

2. Moreover, I see you will magnify yourselves over me, and argue over my destitute condition. Know now that a god has overthrown me, and has enclosed me in his net.

3. Lo, I cry aloud my wrong and I am not answered;

9. *Foliage* seems more probable and appropriate than *verdure*.
11. Doubtful, but nothing better suggests itself.
This seems to form a fitting close to a speech about as unmitigatedly brutal under the circumstances as can well be conceived. One can imagine it inspired directly by Satan himself, with the object of terrifying Ayub into submission to himself.
1. *Stab;* by sound the word is almost *calumniate.* Judge not and you shall not be judged is a *fundamental* rule which is habitually disregarded. Compare (in original) Rom. xiv. 10–12, observing that the WE in verse 12 has a certain emphasis. St. Paul says in fact that this is the course he prefers himself and recommends to others.
3. *My wrong;* the *my* is not expressed in the Hebrew; perhaps it would be best rendered *I shout murder.*

I call for redress and there is no court. My portion is fenced and I cannot pass; and over my paths he will spread darkness.

4. He has stripped me of might, and my head has lost its crown. He will break down my fence and I shall go away, and he will pluck out my ropes like a tree.

5. And he will kindle against me his wrath, and will count me as one of his enemies. His troops came in all at once, and cast up their road to me, and encamped all round my tent.

6. My brother he has removed from my side, and my acquaintance are quite estranged from me. My nearest and dearest have fallen away from me, and those who knew me have forgotten me.

7. The sojourners in my house, and my very slave-girls, turn away and marvel at me, I am become a stranger in their eyes. I call to my servant and he pays no attention to me, though I entreated him with my mouth.

4. *Might;* radical meaning *heaviness, i.e., weight* in counsel, &c., rather than *glory,* the usual rendering.

Ropes; this seems to be the radical meaning, and perhaps if we translated *mast* instead of *tree* the meaning would be clearer; but then we should lose half the simile. Amplifying somewhat " I am like a mast whose stays have been severed, and I shall go by the board like a tree uprooted by the wind." But though Ayub paints his desperate condition so forcibly he still retained the assurance that strength would be supplied him as we shall see a few verses further on.

5. *Cast up their road;* nearly the Latin *munire viam;* they set to work methodically to surmount the difficulties of approach. Commentators seem to think the *troops* referred to are Ayub's calamities, whereas they are evidently the emissaries of Satan who brought them about.

6. Notwithstanding the truly considerate conduct of his three friends at first, as described at the end of chap. ii., and their real desire to help him; they lacked the power to enter into sympathy with him, and have become a byword to this day. Who does not understand the expression *Job's comforters ?*

7. *Marvel;* strictly *think, meditate;* but evidently some such force.

8. My breath is repulsive to my wife, and my notice to the sons of my mother. Nay mere sucklings turned from me, I stood up and they exclaimed at me.

9. All the men of my counsel abhor me and those whom I love turn away from me. My bones stick to my skin and to my flesh, and I have whetted my teeth on my own skin.

10. Incline to me! Incline to me, ye my friends, for the hand of a god has smitten me. Why do you persecute me like the gods, and are not satisfied with my flesh.

11. Who will give that my words should be written down! Let it be granted, and they shall be inscribed in a book; or with an iron graving-tool and with lead let them be cut on the rock for ever.

12. For I know that my Redeemer is the Living God,

---

8. *Sons of my mother;* this is clearly the meaning Gesenius assigned to the passage, and which R.V. adopts.

Exclaimed; the word means to *speak* in the most general sense, here clearly the intention is that children were frightened at seeing him move. Of course the plague of boils with which Satan had smitten him must not be forgotten.

9. *My bones stick to my skin.* Apparently meaning that he cannot move a limb without pain.

Whetted; Gesenius gives the radical meaning *to be smooth,* and his English translator *to make smooth.* The usual rendering is simple rubbish, at the least reflection must shew.

10. *Like the gods;* or rather *quasi deus,* a phrase hardly to be rendered in modern English, but to be understood by what Horace says, " Quem deus vult perdere prius amentat." " Whom the gods would destroy they first deprive of reason." And this was doubtless his deliberate opinion from what he saw of life, and singularly in accord with incidents like the collision of the Victoria and Camperdown on a summer sea in fine weather, by the apparently deliberate action of those on board.

Ayub seems to say he can understand one of the unseen powers not being content with the utter wreck of his affairs and the rendering of his own flesh an encumbrance to him, but that it is inhuman in his brother man to persecute him further.

and at last He will arise on the earth; and the end of the destruction of my skin is this, that in the end I shall see God. Aye! I myself shall see Him, and my eyes shall behold Him and not another; my flesh is perishing with the task.

13. Oh, that you would say, Why persecute him! The root of the matter I have grasped. Turn aside for your own sakes from the face of the sword; for scathing are the turnings of the sword, that you may regard judgment.

12. *Is the Living God;* in the Hebrew simply *lives*, but with a depth of meaning which justifies some amplification in English. *Arise;* or *stand up*, *i.e.*, to redress Ayub's wrongs and discomfit his persecutors.

Whatever larger interpretations this passage may have, if Ayub be regarded as a type of the human race, or of portion of it who have the like faith; it is clear that he used it of himself personally, and moreover was not disappointed of his hope. See the catastrophe of the book.

And not another; apparently meaning that there shall be no possible flaw or mistake about his identity, such as might result from the dissolution of his body.

Flesh; commonly translated *reins*, but Gesenius evidently inclines to the meaning *instrument*, *vessel*, meaning the earthen vessel of this mortal flesh; in which sense σκεῦος is often used in Greek, and it may be added has been similarly misunderstood.

With the task; or more exactly *with my task*. Ayub clearly understood his sufferings, and at least in part the end they were destined to subserve.

13. *The root of the matter I have grasped;* the A.V. seems to have seized the meaning pretty accurately. Ayub prays them to lecture him no further, but believe that he understands his own troubles.

That you may regard judgment; the suggestions here seem very pregnant. (1) That you may remember that there is a tribunal and not lightly incur penalties thereat. (2) That you may beware of hastily forming injurious judgments concerning others, lest the same measure be dealt to you. See what he says before, chap. ix. 12-15, *ante.*

XIV. **A**ND ZOPHAR THE NAAMATHITE replied. And he said: Nevertheless my doubts return, and my feelings are in a state of disturbance and transition. I hear a correction which shames me, and my spirit is at strife with my understanding.

2. Are you aware of this: From all time from the creation of man upon the earth, the exultation of the wicked is transient, and the rejoicing of the impious lasts but a moment?

3. Can his soarings mount to the heavens, or his head penetrate mysteries? Like his own dung he will die to all that is sublime; all that he sees declares to him his own nothingness. Like a dream he will fly away, and they will not attain to it; and he will be chased away like a vision of the night.

4. The eye glances upon him and he is gone, and his place shall behold him no more. His sons will delight in the

1. *My doubts return;* some interval doubtless occurred before anyone spoke after Ayub's tremendous utterance. Afterwards Zophar reverts to what he had said before, see his first great speech, in which he clearly intimates that Ayub seems to him over confident in the presence of the mysteries of the Unseen. The rest of the sentence is somewhat amplified but seems to give the sense of the Hebrew, though not its inimitable brevity.

2. *The wicked;* it seems probable that Zophar means by *the wicked, impious,* not those who are exceptionally wicked, but fallen man at large. In fact he seems to argue that man is not only fallen, but that it is quite out of the question for him to get up; a position amply answered by the history of Enoch and the book he penned.

3. *Penetrate mysteries;* evidently the intention. Clearly Zophar has been taken aback by Ayub's confidence, and has called to mind the esteem in which he had once held him. Only, he seems to say, the sudden termination of such prosperity looks so very much as if Ayub had been found wanting, and guilty of presumption.

Nothingness; Zophar seems to argue that the flesh is manifestly but a perishable garment; the matter of which it is composed is brought under the control of that mysterious thing we call *life* only to be let go again.

4. *He is gone;* this is paraphrase rather than translation, but it seems to give the sense exactly.

D

feeble, and his hands will give up his wealth. His bones are full of childishness, and his kin will lie down in the dust.

5. Lo, evil is sweet to his taste, he will hide it under his tongue; he will treat it gently and will not let it go, and will hold it in his mouth. He has swallowed riches, and shall disgorge them again, God will expel him from possession. The head of serpents will suck, the tongue will slay; I protest.

6. Will he see the rivers, the flowing streams of honey and milk? He will frustrate his own labour, and not enjoy

4. *Give up his wealth;* or perhaps *confess his childishness;* in either case the intention is much the same.

Childishness; Gesenius renders the word *youth, juvenile age,* and translates, " His bones are full of juvenile strength," but the meaning seems rather to be *juvenile weakness, puerility, childishness.*

5. *I protest;* Zophar says that he is not maintaining anything abstruse or singular, but merely what everyone knows. One mistake that seems to have been made about Hebrew poetry is that the sense is necessarily broken at the pauses in the metre; whereas it appears often to be carried on quite independently of them. Robert Browning's poetry is full of instances that illustrate this; take for instance the following lines from his Dramatic Romance,

THE STATUE AND THE BUST.

So, while these wait the trump of doom
How do their spirits pass I wonder
Nights and days in the narrow room?

Still, I suppose, they sit and ponder
What a gift life was, ages ago,
Six steps out of the chapel yonder.

Only they see not God, I know,
Nor all that chivalry of his,
The soldier saints who, row on row,

Burn upward each to his point of bliss;
Since, the end of life being manifest,
He had burned his way thro' the world to this.

I hear you reproach, " But delay was best,
For their end was crime." — Oh, a crime
will do

As well, I reply, to serve for a test

As a virtue golden through and through,
Sufficient to vindicate itself
And prove its worth at a moment's view.

The true has no value beyond the sham :
As well the counter as coin, I submit,
When your table's a hat, and your prize a dram.

Stake your counter as boldly every whit.
Venture as warily, use the same skill,
Do your best, whether winning or losing it,

If you choose to play I — is my principle.
Let a man contend to the uttermost
For his life's set prize, be it what it will !

The counter our lovers staked was lost
As surely if it were lawful coin :
And the sin I impute to each frustrate ghost

Is the unlit lamp and the ungirt loin,
Though the end in sight was a vice, I say
You of the virtue (we issue join)
How strive you ? *De te fabula.*

6. *Milk;* Gesenius gives *curdled milk* as the meaning, the Eastern nations seldom using milk fresh. This has not an attractive sound to English ears, and the Jewish School and Family Bible renders it *clotted cream,* which gives the idea better perhaps for English readers.

the fruits of it; his pay is as it were travail, and he shall not rejoice.

7. Because he crushed and deserted the feeble; he rifled a house and he shall not build one. Because he knew not good faith in his heart he shall not repose in his desire.

8. There was nothing over from his meals, therefore his prosperity shall not endure. In the fulness of his redundancy he shall be in straits; every hand of toil shall come upon him.

9. It shall be for the filling ·of his belly he shall send forth upon him the heat of his anger, and rain it upon them as they sit at meat.

10. He shall flee from a weapon of iron; a copper bow shall transfix him. He drew the sword, and he shall be shut out from honour; lightnings from his own bitterness shall overwhelm him with terrors.

11. Every darkness hid in his treasuries shall devour him; a fire unblown shall rage, the sole tenant in his tent.

8. *There was nothing over from his meals;* compare the injunctions to leave gleanings in the harvest-field, vineyard, &c. Levit. xix. 9, 10.

9. *As they sit at meat;* or *over their food.* Probably to be understood by comparison with Ps. lxxviii. 30, 31.

10. *Copper bow;* perhaps the idea would be conveyed better to English readers by translating *bow of steel,* as is done in A.V., but this would involve manifest sacrifices in other directions.

Be shut out from honour; or more exactly, *He shall withdraw from lifting up,* and so perhaps, *He shall not be raised when he falls.* The word in this verse, which current translations render *body,* appears to be so rendered nowhere else; and the idea that it has this meaning seems to lack foundation.

Lightning . . . terrors. Current translations seem completely at fault here, and to sin alike against grammar and sense. Zophar seems to be contending that each will be treated according to the measure he deals to others; that he who draws the sword shall perish by the sword, and he who deals in bitterness and harshness shall be overwhelmed with terrors, the fruit of his own acts.

11. *A fire unblown;* the meaning evidently is that he will perish through the consequences of his own acts, without machinations on the part of others. Compare the career of the Knight Templar, Brian de Bois Gilbert, in Sir Walter Scott's *Ivanhoe.*

The heavens shall disclose his perversity, and the earth shall bear witness against him. The produce of his house shall be uncovered, swept away in the day of his wrath.

12. This is the lot of the wicked man from the Heaven-abiders, and the portion of those who argue with God.

XV.

AND AYUB replied; and he said: Nay, but hear what I say, and let this reassure you. Bear with me and I will speak, and after I have spoken fool if you please.

2. As for me, am I making complaint to man? And moreover, what if my spirit is impatient? Turn to me and be confounded, and lay your hand upon your mouth. And yet I was careful and timid, and terrors took hold upon my flesh.

3. To what end shall the wicked be removed? Nay,

11. *Bear witness* ; literally *stand up*, but evidently with some such force. Compare the fate of the house built upon the sand, Matt. vii. 26, 27. All that Zophar says in this speech seems cogent enough in the abstract, but the question is whether it had any bearing upon the matter in hand.

1. *Nay but hear* ; or, *Hear attentively* and really, do not merely pretend to hear.

Fool, if you please ; or, *you shall fool, mock, if you please.* Ayub knows that he is not the aggressor. A quarrel cannot be said to exist when all the smiting is done by one party, and the other is only passive under the blows.

2. Ayub seems to contend that impatience of spirit, so long as it finds no outlet in lawless conduct, is no crime. How can he be expected to talk and act as if he had suffered nothing. If it were possible to do so, yet to do it would be to show contempt indeed for the Unseen. Accordingly, in the next word he bids them try to realise what his position really is, and let that awe them into silence. Let them cease to seek the cause of these sufferings in him, and ask themselves how they are to escape destruction.

Be removed; in spite of current translations this is the meaning by Gesenius' Lexicon.

their strength is a fence to them. Their seed shall rise up before their face, at their side ; and their offspring in their sight.

4. Their house is steadfast and unshaken, and the rod of God comes not upon them. Their bull genders without fail, and their cow will calve and not miscarry.

5. They will send forth their progeny like a flock, and their children will dance ; they will go in with timbrel and harp, and rejoice to the sound of the pipe.

6. They spend their days in prosperity, and in a moment Sheol will break them. And they will say to God : Depart from our midst, we delight not in the knowledge of Thy Way. Who is Shaddai that we should be His slaves, and what would it profit us to be in covenant with Him ?

7. Lo, they have no hold on their prosperity ; the counsel of the unrighteous is far from me. How shall the lamp of the unrighteous be extinguished, and their load come upon them ? He will allot them torture in his anger; they will be like straw before the wind, and like chaff, destruction shall carry them off.

8. God will hide their nothingness from their sons; He

---

3. *Their strength is a fence to them ;* it has been said there is no defence against prophecy but to disbelieve it. In fact, the thoughtless and foolish banish Almighty God to Heaven and live in H—l themselves.

6. *In a moment . . . . ;* apparently meaning that they will not be dismayed by the terrors of death, but be cut off unexpectedly, and, as it were, by accident. Ayub is apparently drawing the picture of the happy man according to his friend's ideas, who troubles not himself with thoughts of the Unseen, and is left in peace by it accordingly, and suffered to suppose it has no existence.

Shaddai ; Omnipotent, sufficient.

7. *Torture ;* seems the best rendering, as the root means *twisting.*

Destruction ; Gesenius gives *whirlwind, tempest,* but it seems better to adhere to the radical meaning here.

will repay it to them, and he shall see it, and they shall drink of the wrath of Shaddai.

9. For what is it he delights in in his house, after all? and by the characters of his own inscription they are cut in two. Will he teach the Mighty chastisement, and shall such as he judge heaven-abiders?

10. One will die with his bones sound, his whole being tranquil and secure; his sides are full of fat, and marrow will moisten his bones. And one will die in bitterness of soul, and will not taste good. Together they will lie in the dust, and worms will hide them.

11. Lo, I see your designs and the craft with which you would tear me down. For you say: Where is a princely house? And where the tent, the abode of the wicked? Have you not asked the passer-by the way, for you could not mistake their signs; since the wicked is reserved for a day of calamity, they will flow on to a day of retribution?

12. Who will declare his way to his face, and repay him what he wrought? Assuredly he will pass on to the grave-yard, and his thoughts are fixed upon the tomb; the waves of the river will engulf him. And his end will draw all mankind, and from his face crowds unnumbered. And how will you groan over me with your breath, and your answers remain fallacious!

8. And to Michael He said: Go, Michael, and bind Semiazas and the others with him, who have mixed themselves up with the daughters of mankind and been defiled in their uncleanness; and when their sons are slaughtered and they have seen the destruction of their beloved children, bind them for seventy generations into the valleys of the earth until the day of judgment, until the decision of the age is completed.—*From the Book of Enoch.*

9. *By the characters of his own inscription*, or *graving*; this rendering involves the substitution of a *Resh*, where current impressions read *Daleth*, but the change is very slight, and the sense seems to demand it.

Heaven-abiders, or more exactly *Exalted ones*. Compare I. Cor. vi. 3, and many other passages.

XVI. ND ELIPHAZ THE TEMANITE replied, and he said : Shall a man associate with God as the understanding associate with them ?

2. Does it delight Shaddai that you are righteous, or wound him that you have a perfect cause ? Will he argue with you through fear of you? will he go in with you to judgment ?

3. Has not your wickedness become colossal? And there is no end to your perversity. For you torture your brother without cause, and strip off the clothing of the naked. You have not given the fainting water to drink, and you have withheld food from the hungry.

4. As for man, his arm is the earth; and his true ambition to dwell in it. You have sent widows away empty, and crushed the arm of the bereaved; therefore everything about you is a snare, and terrors shall overwhelm

1. *With them ;* the exact intention here is obscure for it does not appear to whom *them* refers, whether to the gods or to mankind; but the general drift is not difficult to follow.

3. Ayub had maintained in his last speech that the prosperous in this life of the flesh are those who pay no attention to the Almighty and regard not His ways; and anyhow since they end in death their failure is manifest. Eliphaz seems to regard this as a heartless exposure of the woes of mankind, which it is useless to drag into the light; a wanton mockery of human nature and an exposure of its nakedness as it were. Eliphaz seems to be of the very common opinion that mankind ought to be pitied for their misfortunes and treated gently ; whereas the true attitude of the understanding is rather to treat all the troubles of this mortal life as mere childish trifles, which man when he comes to maturity will rise above and forget as he does the mishaps and trials of childhood. Compare I. Cor. xiii. 9-13.

4. *True ambition ;* this is rather paraphrase than translation. *The lifting up of the face* perhaps means rather *prosperity* than *ambition.* Eliphaz contends that he who discharges the duties of this life (as Eliphaz understands them) and dies honoured by his fellows, has fulfilled the intention of his Creator and the object of his existence. This, of course, is precisely what Satan would have fallen man to believe, in order that he may be discouraged from all attempts to get up again and walk.

you in a moment; you shall not see your dark desire, and a flood of waters shall overwhelm you.

5. Is not God High as Heaven? And see, the Head of the Stars how remote He is in His exaltation. And you say, What does God see? Will He reign even to the limits of the nether darkness? Darknesses veil Him and He will not see, and the vault of heaven will run its course.

6. Will you follow the way of the perverse, which men of naught tread? Their way of grasping at the wrong time! The flood will sweep away their foundations. Who say to God, Turn aside from us; and what has Shaddai to do for them? Yet He filled their houses with good. Far from me be the counsel of the unrighteous.

7. The righteous will see and rejoice, and the innocent shall laugh over him. Have not those who have risen up against us been disowned, and has not fire devoured their cords? Dwell, I pray you, with him and be at peace, receive instruction from his mouth, and lay his words to heart.

5. Apparently an allusion to Ayub's contention that those whom the world counts prosperous and praiseworthy are really defying the Almighty and in rebellion against Him. This Eliphaz perverts into a denial of the Reign of God upon earth, quite forgetting that Ayub points to their death as the very sign of the presence and power of His reign.

Will run its course; this seems to be just the force of the verb which Gesenius renders πορεύομαι, *sich ergehen.*

6. *Far from me . . . . . of the unrighteous;* or, *The counsel of the unrighteous is far from me.* The very words Ayub had used in his last speech recur in the Hebrew, and one object of the writer seems to be to shew that the different attitude of the different speakers really results from their occupying different stand-points.

7. *Their cords;* the simile appears to be the same as in Eliphaz's first speech (chap. iv. 9, *ante*), and the key to the understanding of Eliphaz throughout seems to be that he holds as it were a brief for Satan, and argues everything from his point of view.

8. Will you turn again even to Shaddai? You shall be built, you shall remove iniquity from your tent. For He hid precious ores in the dust, and veins of Ophir in the rock ; so let Shaddai be as it were your rock, and silver the object of your labour.

9. For then Shaddai will delight in you, and you will lift up your face to God. You shall make supplication to Him and He will give ear to you, and you shall pay your vows. You shall decide a matter, and it shall stand accordingly, and over your path a shining light.

10. For humble yourselves and you shall command promotion, and he who lowers his eyes shall be helped. He will deliver where there is innocence, and your palms shall be sleeked with winnowed corn.

8. *The object of your labour;* Gesenius gives *weariness, tiring labour,* hence *wealth* derived from labour. Ayub contended in his last speech that temporal prosperity is worthless, and the favour of the Almighty the only thing worth striving for. Eliphaz entreats him to give up so hopeless a position, and treat the Almighty as men treat the rock from which they extract the precious metals, *i.e.,* as quite unfeeling and impersonal, a source of wealth to the industrious, but quite incapable of any sympathy with man.

9. *Shaddai will delight in you;* According to the meaning assigned to the verb by Gesenius, the meaning can hardly be other than " You will be *attractive, alluring,* to Shaddai," just as men and women often think most of those who are utterly careless of their wishes and feelings. To quote the A.V. in fact, Eliphaz exhorts Ayub to *continue in sin that grace may abound.*

Vows; the Hebrew word is almost identical with the Hindustani *nasr* or *nussur,* the offering made by a subject to his king or liege lord in token of allegiance.

10. *Palms shall be sleeked;* the passage is difficult to render satisfactorily, but there seems distinct reference to the idea of *greasing the palm,* a well-known device to propitiate anyone whose goodwill it is desirable to secure.

XVII. AND AYUB REPLIED and he said: Nay, the very day is bitterness, I maintain, my hand represses my sighs.

2. Who will give me to see, and I shall find him, I shall rise to his level. I will set before him my cause, and I will fill my mouth with arguments; I will see the words he will declaim to me, and I will distinguish who is speaking with me.

3. Is there might in the multitude? He will plead my cause; assuredly he will not impose upon me, for then were the upright convicted before him, and I and my cause were consigned to oblivion.

4. Lo, I will go forward and he is not there; and backward, yet I discern him not. On the left is his handiwork, but I see him not; on the right he will hide, and I shall not perceive. Yet he sees the way of my cause, let him prove me and I shall come forth like gold.

5. My foot has seized upon his track; I have observed his way, and I will not turn aside : the commandments of his lips, and I will not give way; for my portion I have laid up the utterances of his mouth.

6. He will unite, and who will make it void, and his soul desired and it will come to pass; for my portion shall be

---

1. *I maintain;* or, *my discourse, i.e.,* this is the substance of what I say. What did Ayub want with winnowed corn if he is robbed of all object in living?

My hand . . . .; i.e., his sighs and lamentations are kept back with an effort, from a sense of their uselessness.

3. *The multitude;* if any one wants sound advice he naturally goes to a specialist. Ayub in fact contends that the way of life is a narrow way, which the multitude shun.

5. This appears to be a categorical reply to Eliphaz's exhortation to make silver the object of his labour.

safe, and with him are myriads such. Therefore at His presence I shall tremble, I shall be attentive and cautious before Him.

7. A god broke my heart and a mighty one struck terror into me; for I shall not be put to silence in the presence of darkness, nor before the throne of gloom.

8. Why? Events are not hidden from Shaddai, and he sees it. His days lack vision! They will remove boundaries; they have carried off flocks and they will tend them. They will drive the ass of orphans, they will tether the ox of widows, they thrust aside the needy from the road; with one consent the poor of the earth hid themselves.

9. See the wild asses of the prairies. They go forth to their occupations in search of pasture, the desert is food for him from his youth; they will reap their provender in the waste and glean in a barren field.

10. They will lodge naked and destitute of clothing, and perchance there is no shelter; the mountains will be wet with showers, and for lack of refuge they will crowd round a rock.

11. They will browse on a deserted field and shun a cultivated one; they walk naked and without clothing, and when hungry they pick up a sheaf. Do wine-casks gleam within their walls, to which they may have recourse when thirsty?

8. *Why;* or strictly, according to Gesenius, *what is taught?* which suits the context admirably.

Events; or, more strictly, *opportunities, crises.* Often we look for help, but none comes, and the crisis seems to pass, yet the Almighty overlooks it not, He sees and knows it all.

His days lack vision! A very pregnant clause, connecting what precedes with what follows, and at the same time pointing the contrast. "Do you think Shaddai sees not? Nay, the blind are those who remove boundaries . . . . "

12. Shall men complain more than an ass, and will you utter cries like a man transfixed and God not be disgusted? This is the way of the enemies of light; they see nothing strange in such conduct, and they do not sit down in their tracks.

13. They will rise at the light; eagerly they will cut the afflicted and needy, and at night they will be like thieves. And their eye commits adultery; it watches for evening to say, No eye will see me; and they set their face in secret.

14. In the dark they break into houses; the day locks them up, they see not the light. For to them the dawn is all one as the shadow of death, for they regard terrors as the shadow of death. Swift is he over the face of the waters, you will curse their guile upon the earth; he will not turn the way of cultivation.

15. Drought and heat together dissipate the snow waters; so does Sheol sinners. Mercy shall forget him,

12. *Be disgusted ;* or more exactly, *impute unsavouriness* to you.
Do not sit down in their tracks ; or in other words, *Do not let the grass grow under their feet.*

14. Compare the words of the well-known glee, "The chough and crow," which considering the nature of the sentiments expressed enjoys a singular popularity.
Swift is he . . . . upon the earth ; there is evidently an elaborate play upon the words in the Hebrew, which it would probably be impossible to translate if one could follow it exactly. Such double meanings are of constant occurrence and often make anything like a satisfactory rendering seem hopeless.

15. *Sinners ;* or, perhaps still better, *duffers.* The figure is drawn evidently from rivers having their sources in lofty mountains capped with snow. The well-known rising of the Nile is due to the melting of the snow on the mountains at its source.
Mercy ; Gesenius says the word has the same meaning as the Greek σπλάγχνα, *i.e., vitals,* the *heart, &c.,* and so the *heart-felt* emotions.

the worm will eat him up, the light shall not remember him, and iniquity shall be broken on a tree.

16. Evil is barren and shall not have offspring, and brutal dumbness shall not prosper. It draws mighty ones by its strength, it rises and will not trust aught living. He will give it confidence and it will lean, and his eye is upon their road.

17. They rose a little and for him they had no existence and melted away; they are gathered in the common fashion, and they will gather them like the head of a branch. And if it is otherwise now, who will convict me of falsehood, and bring my words to nothing?

XVIII. AND BILDAD THE SHUHITE replied; and he said: Does He deal in parables and terrors? He is working out salvation in his fortresses.

2. Is there any counting his troops, and upon whom will His light not arise? And how shall man be just before God, and how shall one born of woman be clean?

---

15. *Broken on a tree;* apparently meaning it will be crucified, or as we say will come to the gallows.

16. *Brutal dumbness;* this is rather paraphrase than translation, but seems to be the intention, viz., that man if inarticulate through ignorance or indifference is no better than the beasts which perish.

17. *A little;* apparently the meaning is that the ordinary man rises so slightly above the brutes that for the Almighty the difference is imperceptible.

Ayub's contention seems to be that mankind are all astray, and the height of their ambition is to die at a good old age. Whereas for Ayub anything transitory is not worth having.

1. *Terrors;* apparently in the sense of *bugbears, bogey stories.*

3. Look even to the moon and she shines not, and the stars are not clean in his sight; much more is man beguiled, and the son of Adam a worm.

4. AND AYUB REPLIED; and he said: How hast thou helped the strengthless, and succoured an arm devoid of might! How hast thou counselled one without skill, and taught wisdom to the multitude!

5. How hast thou told forth words! and what wit has proceeded out of your mouth! Shall spectres writhe beneath; the waters and the things that live in them?

6. Sheol is naked before Him, and hell has no covering. He stretches the North over empty space, He hangs the earth upon nothing. He binds up water in His clouds, and the vapour is not rent under them.

7. Veiling the face of his throne he spreads clouds over it; ordinances and festivals over the face of the waters as far as where light ends in darkness.

8. The pillars of heaven will be smitten and wonder at his rebuke. By his power he restrains the sea, and by his skill he stirs it to its limits.

9. By his breath the heavens shine, his hand made the

---

3. *Shines not;* the moon of course is only visible to us by the light she reflects, and can hardly be visible at all outside the solar system, for we need telescopes to see the satellites of other planets in our own system, and have never seen even the planets of any other system.

5. *Wit;* or making the clause a mere exclamation, *wind, breath, i.e.,* sound without sense, pointless truisms. To Ayub's contention that the ordinary scheme of three-score years and ten of troublous existence not worth calling life, closed by a home in the graveyard, is a lot it is impossible to covet or even to think of with patience; Bildad replies apparently that it leads to something better after death; in fact, he justifies the ordinary idea of man's lot, that he passes to heaven through the gate of physical death. This is easily refuted by the simple question, To what end then the Resurrection? and Ayub laughs the position to scorn.

serpent to writhe in flight. Lo, these are beginnings of his road; but what whispered word is heard of him, and the thunder of His Might who shall abide?

XIX. AND AYUB CONTINUED HIS PARABLE and said: The Living God has taken away my cause and Shaddai has embittered my life. For all the while my breath is in me and divine spirit in my nostrils, my lips shall not speak perversity nor my tongue mutter negligently.

2. Far be it from me to justify you; till I die I will not put away my integrity from me. On my uprightness I have taken fast hold, and will not let it go, my heart shall not pluck off from my day.

3. Let him who opposes me be as the wicked, and my adversary as those who turn aside. For what stay have the impious? For he will break in pieces; for God will draw out his soul.

4. Will God hear his cry when distress comes upon him? Will he delight himself in Shaddai? Will he call upon God at all times?

5. I will cast you into the hand of God; I will not hesitate to declare what is with Shaddai. Lo, you all know,

9. Beginnings; or properly *extremities*, meaning either the ends from His side, or the beginnings from the human stand-point; sign-posts as it were to point the way into the Unseen Universe.

2. *My heart shall not pluck off from my day;* apparently meaning that his heart should justify his whole life to itself, which is precisely the meaning Gesenius gives to the passage, " My heart shall not reproach me as to any day of my life."

3. *Draw out his soul,* or *breath, i.e.,* from his body as from a sheath, so that his body will expire.

every one of you, why you are wasting your breath in this fashion.

6. This respect of persons is hateful to God, and those who intimidate will receive their portion from Shaddai. Even if his sons are multiplied it is for the sword, and his offspring shall not be satisfied with bread; those who survive will be overwhelmed by death, and his widows will not weep.

7. Though he heap up silver like dust, and prepare raiment like foam; he shall prepare and the righteous will wear, and the innocent will divide the silver.

8. He builds a house like the moth, and like a garden-watcher's booth. Rich he will lie down, and it will not be gathered; he opened his eyes and it is gone.

9. Terrors like waters met him, by night whirlwind carried him off. Cold will lift him up and he will go, and he will be swept away from his place.

10. He will hurl upon him and will not spare; from his hand flight shall flee. He will rattle their own hands against them, and will whistle him from his place.

11. For there is a vein for silver, and a place for gold, where they will wash it out. Iron is got from earth, and copper is smelted from stone. He sets a limit for darkness, and all perfection he searches out.

12. Darkness is a stone, and so is the shadow of death; a torrent that breaks over the stranger. Those who lose foothold lack manhood and staunchness.

13. THE EARTH! Out of her grows food. Underneath she is spinning like fire. Her stones are the home of the sapphire, and her dust is gold.

14. THE WAY! No rapacious one knows it, nor has

vulture's eye spied it out. The sons of pride never trod it, lion never passed by it.

15. At a precipice it stretches out its hand. It overturns mountains from the roots. Among stones it cleaves rivers, and its eye sees every difficulty. It binds up rivers that they flow not. And secrets it expels like light.

16. But whence shall Wisdom be acquired, and where now is the abode of Understanding?

17. Man knows not its price, and indeed it was never acquired by those who dwell on the earth. The Sky says, It is not in me; and the Sea says, it is not with me.

18. The deepest mines never yielded it, and silver shall not be weighed in exchange for it. The treasures of Ophir shall not be weighed against it, nor gems of price most finely wrought.

19. Gold and diamonds are no measure of its value, and its price is a frame purified in the fire.

20. Sublimity and icy grandeur—talk not of them; and drag for Wisdom rather than for pearls.

21. The topaz of Ethiopia shall not compare with it; it shall not be weighed against unalloyed treasure.

22 Whence then shall Wisdom find entrance, and where now is the abode of Understanding?

23. Nay, it has been hidden from every living eye, and escaped the ken of the birds of heaven. Hell and Death say, We have heard the fame of it with our ears.

24. GOD discerns its road, and HE sees its abode, for HE looks to the extremities of the earth, HE sees under all the heavens. Even to fashioning a gauge for the wind, and poising the waters by measure.

25. By His contrivance there is a law for the rain, and a

E

road for the thunder-bolt. THEN he saw it, and he will utter it; he prepared it and searched it out.

26. AND SAID TO MAN: Lo, the fear of the Lord is Wisdom; and to depart from evil is Understanding.

XX. AND AYUB CONTINUED HIS PARABLE, and said: Who will set me as in the months before, as in the days when God kept watch over me!

2. With the light of His lamp upon me, my head turned to His light, I walked the darkness.

3. Such as I was in the days of my harvest, with the favour of God over me for a tent; while yet Shaddai was my stay, and my boys about me; when I washed my steps in milk, and the rock poured me out streams of fatness.

4. When I went forth to the gate, the city came about me. To stand up in the assembly was like sitting at ease.

5. The boys saw me and hid themselves, and the grey-headed arose and stood; the nobles stopped in their talk, and laid their hand upon their mouth; the mouth of rulers was stilled, and their tongue stuck in their jaws.

6. When the ear heard me it became attentive; and the eye saw me and called me to witness. For I soothed the afflicted when they cried for help, the orphan and the help-

---

25. *THEN;* By comparison with a later passage, as well as by the context, it would appear that reference is intended to the tremendous catastrophe then fresh in men's minds. Ayub seems to intimate that mankind had not laid to heart the lesson of the Flood, and were going on in the same careless way which brought that catastrophe upon them. Compare chap. xxiv. 10, *sq.*

less; the blessings of the perishing came upon me, and I gave the heart of the widow relief.

7. I put on righteousness and it clothed me like a robe, and my judgment was a turban. Eyes to the blind and feet to the lame was I—a father to the needy; and the case I understood not I searched it out. And I broke the teeth of the vicious, and made him drop the prey from his mouth.

8. And I said: I shall breathe out my life near my nest, and I shall multiply my days as the sand. My root is open to the waters, and the dew will rest upon my boughs.

9. My heart was fresh within me, and my bow was renewed in my hand. To me they gave ear; and waited and kept silence for my counsel. After I had spoken they did not renew the discussion, and my words fell like dew upon them.

10. They awaited me as the rain, and opened wide their mouth for the latter rain. I would laugh at them and they could not bear it, and the light of my countenance did not cause them to fall.

11. I pioneered the road for them, and sat at their head; and dwelt like a king among his troops, as one who sympathises with the distressed.

6. *Gave relief;* or more exactly, *caused to sound, vibrate.* Compare—
 "Home they brought her warrior dead,
  She nor moaned nor uttered sigh;
  All her maidens watching said,
  She must weep or she must die."
In this passage we get some insight into what Ayub meant by *righteousness.* He describes his practice, which his hearers must have known very well to have been the very reverse of all that men commonly practise. The source of Ayub's confidence, in fact, is that he had habitually and systematically supplied the need of his brother man. He had not done it by fits and starts, or under pressure, as it were; but freely and spontaneously, as soon as the need came under his ken.

12. And now they laugh at me who are less than I in age, whose fathers I would have scorned to set among the dogs of my flock. Nay, what can the strength of their hands profit me, seeing they can complete nothing?

13. In want and hard penury they flee into the desert of yesternight's tempest and desolation; plucking salads from the bushes, and roots of broom for food.

14. They will be driven from the midst—they will shout at them as at a thief—to the horrid glens, to dwell in holes scraped in the dust and in caves.

15. They will bray among the bushes, they will gather under the thorn trees; the offspring of fools, yea, nameless children, they were driven with scoffs from the land. And now I am become their song, and I am their scoff.

16. They loathed me; they fled away from me; and in my presence they hid not their disgust. For he has loosed his cord and overthrown me, and they cast off restraint in my presence.

17. On the right hand children arise; they push away my feet, and cast up roads to me for their burdens. They have torn up my ways, they further my ruin; there is no help in them.

---

12. *Seeing they can complete nothing;* this is the meaning Gesenius assigns to the passage, and apparently with good reason. It is not, in whom *old age* is perished, but in whom *completion* has perished; *i.e.*, who cannot attain to maturity themselves, nor acquire the skill necessary to do anything thoroughly and completely. The Jewish School and Family Bible renders "Whom successful accomplishment faileth."

16. *Loosed his cord and overthrown me;* the metaphor seems to be that of an archer, either loosing the cord in discharging the arrow, or slacking the string when he lays the bow aside for a time.

17. *Children; offspring* of beasts, says Gesenius, but the word seems perfectly general. R.V. renders it *the rabble,* and this seems to be pretty nearly the intention.

18. Like a wide breach they burst in; with tempest above them they rolled in; terrors have turned upon me. My dignity has passed like a wind, and my safety has departed like the shadow of a cloud.

19. And now my soul is poured upon me; days of affliction have seized upon me. Darkness from above has penetrated my bones, and my torments have no cessation.

20. By repeated violence my clothing is searched; He will bind my shirt over my mouth. He has cast me in the mire, and I shall be made like dust and ashes.

21. I may cry out to Thee, and Thou wilt not answer me; I stood up, and Thou ponderest over me. Thou art become cruel to me; with relentless hand Thou layest snares for me.

22. Thou wilt lift me up; upon the wind Thou wilt cause me to ride; and Thou wilt dissolve all my counsel. For I have seen death. Thou wilt turn me; and there is a house appointed for all living.

23. Assuredly He will not put forth His hand upon ruins; is there deliverance for them in His calamity?

24. Shall I not bewail him whose day is hard; vex my soul over the wretched? For I expected good and evil came upon me; I waited for light and darkness came.

25. My heart burned and had no rest; days of affliction

---

20. *He will bind* . . . ; the intention seems to be quite missed in modern translations. Quite literally it runs, " He will bind me my shirt on the mouth," apparently meaning that his outcries and remonstrances will be checked or disregarded.

22. *There is a house appointed for all living*; apparently Ayub expresses his confidence that the Almighty provides shelter and all things needful for all who LIVE in any sense worth so calling, and does not turn them back to dust. It was only after Adam stood self-convicted of transgression that he was told, " Dust thou art, and to dust thou shalt return."

forestalled me. I walked in gloom, without sunshine; I stood up in the assembly and asked for help.

26. I have become the brother of jackals and the companion of owls. My skin is sunburnt from exposure, and my bones are on fire through neglect.

27. My harp has become a dirge; and my pipe a voice of lamentation. I have made a covenant with my eyes, and why should I notice a maid? What is the portion of God from above, and the inheritance of Shaddai from the heights?

28. Are not burdens for the perverse, and alienation for the workers of vanity? Will not HE see my road and record every step?

29. If I have walked hand in hand with iniquity, or my foot has hastened to fraud, God will weigh me in a true balance, and will confound my integrity.

30. If my steps have turned out of the way, and my heart has walked after my eye, and if any spot has stained my hands; I shall sow and another will eat, and my descendants will be rooted out.

31. If my heart has been ensnared over a woman, and I have laid wait at my neighbour's door; my wife will grind for another, and others will kneel to her. For this is premeditated, and this is an actionable offence; for this is fire that will consume to destruction, and will root out all my increase.

32. Did I reject the cause of my servant, or of my handmaid, when they contended with me? What then shall I do when God arises, and when He visits me what shall I reply? Did not He who fashioned me in the womb fashion him? And did not One create us in the womb?

33. Have I kept back from the feeble their desire, and caused the eye of the widow to pine? Have I eaten my

morsel alone, and the destitute not eaten of it? Nay, from my youth he twined about me as if I were his father, and from my mother's womb I would be her stay.

34. If I saw a wanderer destitute of clothing, and a needy one had no covering, did not his loins bless me, and would he not be warmed with the fleece of my sheep?

35. Have I shaken my hand at the orphan, when I saw help for me in the gate? My limbs will drop from my shoulders, and my arm will be broken from its socket. For terror is upon me, the dread of God; and for fear of Him I I can do nothing.

36. Have I made hoarded gold my strength, or called treasure my confidence? Have I rejoiced in the multitude of my resources, or because my hand had acquired great possessions? Have I looked upon the sun when he shone, or blessed the moon that she held her course? And would my heart open to them in secret, and my hand be laid to my mouth? This, too, were criminal perversity, for I should be ignoring Him who is Lord over them.

37. Have I rejoiced at the calamity of my enemy, and roused myself when evil befell him? I refused to give my mouth to sin, to demand his life with a curse. Did not the men of my tent say, Who will give of his meat? We are not satisfied! The stranger shall not pass the night in the open air; I will open my door to the traveller.

38. Have I covered my faults like Adam, to bury my perversity in my bosom; that I should fear the strictures of

33. *Her stay*; *i.e.*, the widow's stay, see what goes before.

35. *Shaken my hand at*; in threat, says Gesenius, but more probably simply in negation; the gesture is as common in the East as the shaking of the head with the same intent. *When . . . help . . . in the gate;* apparently meaning, When I should have had public opinion on my side.

the crowd, and the contempt of the people should break me? And shall I be confounded? Shall I not go outside the door?

39. Who will have patience to hear me! Lo, my point is: Shaddai will fashion me, and man will set down the record of my case. Will I not take it upon my shoulder? I will bind it like a crown upon my head. From the record of my steps I will demonstrate that it is so; I will bring it before the Ruler.

40. Will my land cry out against me, or her furrows weep in concert? Have I eaten her strength without silver, or caused distress to her lords. Under wheat thorns will spring up, and under barley stink-weed. The words of Ayub are ended.

XXI. AND THOSE THREE MEN ceased their answers to Ayub because he was righteous in his own eyes.

2. And the anger of Elihu, the son of Barachel, the Buzite of the tribe of Ram, was kindled. Against Ayub was his anger kindled, because he justified his life rather than the Unseen Powers. And against his three friends his wrath burned, inasmuch as they found no answer, and yet exclaimed against Ayub.

3. And Elihu had waited for Ayub while he was speaking,

---

40. *Will my land cry out?* St. Paul says, There are, it may be, so many voices in the Universe, *and nothing voiceless.* To credit inanimate objects with indifference because they betray no sign of feeling, is merely to shew the ignorant heartlessness of childhood.

Caused distress to her lords; more exactly *caused her lords* (*i.e.*, the possessors of the land, the husbandmen) *to pant* with exertion in order to supply my requirements.

because they were older than he in years; and Elihu saw that there was no answer in the mouth of those three men, and his wrath burned.

4. And Elihu, the son of Barachel the Buzite, made answer and said: I am young in years and you are grey-headed, wherefore I was afraid and durst not declare my opinion before you.

5. I said, Days shall speak, and multiplied years will teach wisdom; surely there is spirit in man, and the breath of Shaddai instructs them; the multitudes will not be wise, but the grey-headed will discern judgment.

6. Wherefore I say, Listen to me; I will pronounce what I see, even I. I have waited for your words, and bent my ears to catch your wisdom while you sought for utterance.

7. Yea, I saw your meaning, and lo, there is none to confute Ayub, or who answered his words, among you. You surely will not say: We have achieved wisdom; God, not man, has overthrown him!

8. Now he did not address his discourse to me, and I will not reprove him with words like yours. They were confounded; they made no reply; they found nothing to say. And I waited; for they spoke not. For they halted; they spoke no more.

9. I will speak; even I. I will declare in turn what I see; even I. For I am full of utterance. The spirit within me distresses me. Lo, my belly is like wine unopened; like new wine-skins, it is ready to burst.

10. I will speak and it will give me vent; I will open my lips and declaim. I will not display the countenance of a man; and I shall not seek to please the race of Adam, for I

do not know how.   I flatter but little; my Maker will bear me out.

11.   Wherefore hear, I pray you oh Ayub, the prelude of my words; and listen to all my discourse. Lo, now I have opened my mouth; my tongue has begun to move in my mouth.

12.   My heart shall direct my words, and what I perceive my lips shall set forth carefully. The breath of God has formed me, and the spirit of Shaddai will quicken me. If you are able to confute me, range yourself before me and take your stand.

13.   Lo, I am in God's stead as you said; I too am a creature of clay. Behold, my terror shall not scare you nor my dignity oppress you.

14.   Assuredly you spoke in my hearing, and I heard the sound of words : I AM PURE, VOID OF TRANSGRESSION; I AM UPRIGHT AND THERE IS NO PERVERSITY IN ME. LO, HE is seeking alienation from me; He counts me for his enemy; He watches all my ways.

15.   Lo, this is not right. I will answer you that God is greater than man.

16.   To what end will you maintain against Him that He answers none of your words? For God will speak once, and will pay no attention a second time.

17.   In dreams, visions by night, when deep sleep has fallen on men and they are asleep in bed; then He will uncover the ears of men, and on the instructions He gives He

---

13. *I too am a creature of clay ;* Gesenius translates, " I too am nipped off from clay," and explains the figure as taken from the action of the potter nipping off a lump of clay for the purpose of setting it on the wheel.

will set a seal; that He may divert man from creating, and He will hide exaltation from man.

18. He keeps back his soul from destruction, and his life from passing in front of the bolt. And He will correct him with pains upon his bed, and multiply his rigours continually; till his food stinks in his nostrils, and his soul loathes hunger.

19. His flesh wastes away because of the vision, and his bones, before unseen, are exposed to view; and his soul draws near to destruction, and his life to the destroyers.

20. Is there a messenger for him, an interpreter; one of a thousand, to show man his duty? Then He will pity him and will say: Release him from going down to the pit, I have found an excuse.

21. His flesh will become fresher than a boy's and he will return to the days of his youth. He will pray to God and He will be gracious to him, and he will see His face amid acclamations.

22. And He will restore to man his rightousness; He will visit mankind, and will say: I made a mistake, and perverted the right, and was not fair to him. Release his soul from going down to the pit, and his life shall look upon the light.

17. *Exaltation*; apparently here in the sense of *promotion*, rather than pride. Elihu seems to contend that man was not intended to excel and will not be allowed to do so. Yet the other sense of exaltation, viz., *pride*, is not to be excluded, as we may see by the case of Nebuchadnezzar, as recorded by Daniel.

18. *Rigours*; the root means *strength, hardness*, and hence the word often means "bones." There is a similar use of the word in xx. 21, where the Jewish School and Family Bible translates *strong hand*.

22. The Hebrew Scriptures often represent God as repenting of what he has done, as when He repented that He had made man upon the earth; and after the flood as repenting that He had wrought the destruction, and making a covenant with Noah and his seed that they might not fear a repetition of the Deluge. See also Jerem. viii. 4, and xxvi. 13. A.V. or R.V.

23. Lo, all these things will God work twice, three times, with a man; to deliver his soul from the pit into light, the light of the living.

24. Attend, oh, Ayub, and listen to me; keep silence and I will speak. If you have anything to say, reply to my words, for I desire your justification. If you have nothing, listen to me. Keep silence, and I will teach you wisdom.

XXII. AND ELIHU CONTINUED, and said: Attend to my words, ye wise men, and ye sages lend me your ears; for the ear will try discourse, and the mouth will taste food.

2. We will put judgment to the test for ourselves; we will search understanding for ourselves what is good.

3. For Ayub says: I have been righteous and God has taken away my judgment. Have I lied about my case, a man shot down without transgression!

4. What man, like Ayub, will drink scorning like water, and go in company with the workers of vanity, and walk with men of disorder?

5. For he says, Man shall not abide if he delights himself in the Unseen Powers. Therefore attend to me, ye men of sense.

---

3. *Taken away my judgment;* or perhaps *removed my case, i.e.,* to a higher court. Ayub had expressed his confidence that the Almighty would arise and justify himself. See xiii. 12, *ante.*

5. *Man . . . Powers;* or perhaps, *Man cannot continue to delight himself . . .* The usual rendering seems to give the meaning pretty well, except that it does not give the force of the Hebrew plural, *Aleim* or *Elohim;* compare I. Cor. viii. 5.

6. Far be evil from God, and perversity from the Almighty! For the works of man He will requite to him, and according to a man's ways He will see him repaid. Assuredly then God will not foster disorder nor the Almighty pervert judgment.

7. Who overlooks His management of the earth, and who set in order the habitable globe? If He shall set His heart upon him, collect upon him his spirit and his breath; all flesh will expire together, and man will return to dust: and if you will attend to Understanding, hear this which is the matter of my discourse.

8. Nay further! Can one who hates justice govern? And will you condemn the Just and Great; tell a king he is profitless, and nobles they are evil? Such as lift not up the face of leaders, and repudiate not the wealthy in the presence of the feeble? When everything is the work of His hand!

9. In a moment they will die, and arrows by night will strike down a people, and mighty ones will pass by and be removed without hand. For His eye is upon man's way, and He will see his every step; there is no darkness nor shadow of death where the workers of vanity may be hidden.

10. For He will not put upon man repeatedly that he

8. *Lift not up the face of leaders;* apparently meaning that they do not display the dignity and ability which it is incumbent on leaders to manifest at all times.

9. *Strike down a people;* apparently alluding to catastrophes like the destruction of Sodom, or of Sennacherib's army. The Deluge, itself, then a recent event, was doubtless preceded by striking examples as well as by the preaching of Noah.

10. Contrast with this what St. Paul says, II. Cor. v. 10, viz., that all who are of his mind must appear before the bar where the Christ stands to plead our cause; expressly in order to receive according to what he did in the body.

should go to God for trial. Mighty ones may vociferate, but there is no investigation, and their juniors will stand up in their place.

11. Therefore He will disown their works. He has brought night and they will be broken in pieces; He has chastised them under unrighteous ones instead of under the discerning.

12. Wherefore? Because they turned aside from following Him, and did not attend to any of His ways; to bring up to Him the complaints of the feeble. He will hear the outcry of the feeble.

13. When He gives rest, who will make disturbance? And when He hides His face, who will go to Him, either on behalf of a nation or on behalf of an individual; because of a king who is a profane fellow, a snare of the people?

14. For to God one should say: I was at fault; I am not wilfully perverse. That I see not, shew Thou. If I wrought perversity I will not add to it. Did he recompense according to Thy mind? It is for Thee to reject; for Thou puttest to the test, not I. And who can see anything?

15. Men of heart will say to me; and hear me, oh, wise man. Ayub has not spoken intelligently, and his words are thoughtless.

16. My Father, let Ayub be tried to the uttermost about his answers to men of naught; for he will add defection to his mistake; he will clap his hands among us, and will multiply his words to God.

---

16. *To God;* this is the force of the preposition, not *against,* as in modern English translations. This is contrary alike to the use of the preposition and to the sense of the passage.

XXIII. AND ELIHU CONTINUED, and said: Did you count this for discernment? Did you say, I am more righteous than God? For you said: What shall it profit Thee? How shall I be useful through failure?

2. I will find you a reply, and answer your friends to boot. Look to the heavens and see, and behold the sky exalted above you.

3. If you have erred, what will you do to Him? And multiply your defection, how will you affect Him?

4. If you are righteous, what will you give Him? Or what will He accept at your hand? It is to men like yourself that you are evil, and to the sons of Adam that you are righteous.

5. From the multitude of the oppressors they will cry out, they will complain because of the arm of the multitude. And none says, Where is God, my Maker, Who gives songs by night? Who teaches us more than the beasts of the earth, and will instruct us beyond the birds of heaven.

6. There will they cry out, and He will not send answer to wretches from the presence of Majesty. Assuredly God will not listen to vanity, and the Almighty will not pay attention to it.

7. Still less when you say: Thou wilt not look upon it. There is a tribunal before Him, and you will dance attendance upon it. And the present situation is due to the fact that there is no visitation at present; and He does not look from sheer pride of power.

8. And Ayub caught his breath and compressed his lips, and managed to keep back useless utterance. And Elihu added further, and said:

9. Have patience with me a little, and I will declare to you; for yet again God gives utterance. I will proclaim what I see from my position in the distance, and to my deeds I will ascribe rectitude. For assuredly my words are not deceitful, but a summing up of conclusions with thee.

10. Lo, God is Great, and the great will not reject the stout of heart. He will not protect a rogue, and He will give judgment for the feeble; He will not withdraw His eye from the righteous.

11. Kings are for the throne, and he will cause them to sit in glory, and will protect them; and, if fetters can bind, the feeble will be caught in the noose.

12. And He will declare to them their deeds, and their transgressions how insolent they are become. And He will bare their ears to discipline, and bid them turn from vanity.

13. If they will hear and obey Him, they will spend their days in prosperity and their years in delights; and if they will not listen, the bolt will light upon them, and they will perish unawares.

14. The impious of heart will lay up wrath, they shall not be at large, for He will bind them. Their soul will die in youth, and their life by the holy. He will deliver the feeble in his need, and will bare their ears in affliction.

9. *Yet again—utterance*; or more exactly, *God has yet words to speak.*
A summing up of conclusions; this seems to be the intention. The ordinary rendering, "One perfect in knowledge is with thee," is contrary alike to the construction and to Elihu's whole attitude."

11. *Protect them*; or, more exactly, *hedge, fence.* Compare Shakespeare: "There's such divinity doth *hedge* a king that treason can but peep to what it would." *Hamlet, Act iv. sc. 5.*

13. *The bolt will light upon them*; or, more exactly, *They will light upon the bolt, pass in front of it* and so be struck down; or, *pass over* (*i.e.,* perish) by it.

14. *By the holy*; this seems the intention, modern translations notwithstanding. LXX translate ὑπ' ἀγγέλων; compare chap. xix. 1-10, *ante.*
Bare their ears; *i.e.,* cause them to hear, open their ears.

15. Moreover, if He had dealt with you by the mouth of an enemy, enlargement, not constraint, would have resulted ; and your table would have been spread with fatness. If you have made out a bad case, case and sentence will accord.

16. For beware lest He deal with you summarily and give you not repeated pardon. Will He value your wealth ? Not precious ore, nor all the vigour of might.

17. Will you pant for night, for peoples to rise up beneath them ? Take heed lest you turn to nihilism, for this is the matter on which you were examined as to your answer.

18. Lo, God will be exalted according to His Might. Who as He has power to lash ? Who will visit upon Him his way ; and who say, Thou hast done injustice ? Remember to magnify His acts which mankind celebrate. All men look to Him ; mankind will regard Him from afar.

19. Lo, God is Great, and we cannot tell His years nor search them out. When He has collected drops of water, He will express rain from His clouds which will fall ; showers will drop on man abundantly. How much more will He

15. *Dealt with* ; Gesenius gives the meaning *to provoke, instigate* ; and though he would give it a different sense here he gives no sufficient reason. It occurs again a little lower down, and a sense has to be found suitable to the context in both places.

16. *Summarily* ; Gesenius thinks " chastisement " is the meaning here, but gives the radical meaning *to clap the hands*, and the intention seems to be rather : " Beware lest He get sick of you and think only of how to get rid of you." The passage seems to have puzzled translators, and yet if the root meanings given by Gesenius are attended to, the sense emerges pretty clearly.

17. *Nihilism* ; this word by derivation gives just the sense of the Hebrew word, and expresses the intention of the speaker admirably in English.

discern the dissemination of darkness, any clatter in his tabernacle.

20. Lo, He spreads His light above Him, and covers the source of the waters; for thereby He holds the peoples in subjection, and gives food to the multitudes.

21. Over the hollows He spreads light, and commissions it against those who oppose Him. He will manifest upon him his evil-doing; the wrath they have purchased, upon the wicked. Nay, it is at this my heart trembles and leaps from her seat.

22. Listen! Listen! To the thunder of His voice, and the uproar that proceeds from His mouth.

23. He darts it forth under all the heavens, and His light to the extremities of the earth. After Him will roar a voice, His Majesty will thunder audibly; and He will not supplant those who attend to His voice.

24. God will roar with His voice; He has wrought wonders of sublimity, and we will not see. For to the snow

---

19. *The dissemination of darkness;* apparently meaning the spreading of nihilistic ideas, but with a play on the word rendered darkness, which as an architectural term means *threshold steps.* *Any clatter in his tabernacle;* Elihu seems to warn Ayub not to bring upon himself the anger of the Master of the tent by unseemly noise or quarrelling with his fellow-servants. The Almighty, he seems to say, pays little attention to the deeds of men so long as they do their appointed work quietly and in an orderly manner; just as a man does not trouble himself about what his servants do amongst themselves, so long as they pitch and remove his tent as he requires; but if they make a row and disturb him he will be likely to punish the offender against his repose.

20. *The source of the waters;* Not " the bottom of the sea," as modern translators render, but the *root, i.e.,* the source, origin, from which the waters spring; the fountains or storehouses from which He waters the earth and renders it fruitful.

22. *Listen . . . to the uproar;* Elihu seems to warn Ayub to open his ears, not to any physical sound, but to that which only the opened ear can hear.

He will say BE EARTH, and torrents of rain, aye torrents of multiplied rain, declare His might.

25. On the hand of every man He will set a seal, that all mankind may know His acts; and life will enter her lair, and in her dwellings she will abide.

26. From His chamber will go forth the whirlwind, and from the winds whatsoever befalls. From the breath of God proceeds ice, and an expanse of water becomes cast-iron.

27. Moreover, for watering purposes He will let fall the mist; His light will disperse the clouds. And thus on all sides are complicated contrivances for working all that He appoints them upon the face of the inhabited earth. Whether for the rod, or for His earth, or for blessing, we shall come in contact with Him.

28. Hear this, oh, Ayub. Stand and shew yourself attentive to the wondrous acts of God. If you will look when

---

24. BE EARTH; the allusion is evidently to the deluge, then a comparatively recent event. The *snow*—or perhaps rather *ice*—referred to was evidently not part of the earth, and can hardly be anything, but the waters above the firmament; which on their removal beyond the atmosphere were congealed into ice and sent spinning round the earth as satellites forming a ring system like that of Saturn.

26. *From the winds;* or, more exactly, *from the winnowing-fans.* The idea is evidently to express that what appears chance or accident to us is no more accidental in reality than the wind before which the husbandman sifts his grain in order that the chaff may be separated from it. The so-called winnowing-fan is not used to make the wind, but as a basket or shovel for the mingled chaff and grain; which are thrown up into the air, or sifted from a height, so that the wind may effect the separation.

Ice; or perhaps rather *congelation.*

Cast-iron; or more exactly *cast* like metal, glass, &c. Gesenius gives the meaning carefully, but singularly enough misses its applicability to this passage.

27. *Let fall the mist;* or, in the language of modern science, *precipitate* the invisible watery vapour.

God gives them their instructions, His clouds will be brilliant with light.

29. If you will look to the poising of cloud, there are miracles of perfect wisdom. How are your clothes oppressive in sultry weather, when the sun's heat pours upon the earth?

30. Will you help Him to pound to dust the hardened as if they were a cast mirror? Shew as what we shall say to Him; I will not range myself on the side of darkness.

31. Should one speak to Him as I speak? Should man say: He will eat me up and now there is no seeing bright light. This is mere dust, and when spirit passes we shall be quickened.

32. Shall gold come forth from gloom? To God Stupendous Majesty! SHADDAI!! We shall not find Him. GREAT in might and judgment; and multiplication of righteousness will not accomplish it. Therefore, have mankind seen HIM? Not the most understanding of heart shall see Him.

---

30. *We shall*; or, more literally, *they will*, but apparently in the impersonal sense expressed in French by *on*. *On reviendra;* one will return, *i.e.*, a return will take place, without specifying who will return.

A cast mirror; not "a molten looking-glass," for anything molten is fluid, but a mirror of cast-iron, so to speak, or rather not iron, but speculum, metal or glass, both of them very refractory and brittle substances. The idea is that of smashing up for the melting-pot a defective casting.

31. *We shall be quickened;* or, more literally, *it will quicken them*, apparently in the impersonal sense already remarked upon: *quickening will take place*. This in fact is the very attitude of St. Paul, who taught that this mortal life is mere death, and the only thing worth striving for is resurrection out of it.

XXIV. AND JEHOVAH SPOKE TO AYUB from the midst of the tempest, and said: WHO IS THIS THAT DARKENS COUNSEL BY WORDS DEVOID OF SENSE?

2. Gird now thy loins like a man; and I will question thee, and do thou shew Me. Where wast thou when I founded the earth? Proclaim if thou knowest understanding.

3 Who appointed her dimensions, if thou knowest? Or who stretched the line upon her? On what have her foundations been sunk? Or who laid her corner-stone? When all the stars of dawn sang in concert, and all the sons of the gods applauded.

4. And who fenced in the Sea with gates; what time he burst forth, issuing from the womb? When I appointed him· cloud for clothing, and thick mist for a swathing band. And 𝔍 broke over him My established order, and 𝔍 set bars and gates, and said: THUS FAR shalt thou come, and no further; and HERE shall thy rolling might be stayed.

1. It is worthy of note that the catastrophe is to each of those concerned in accordance with his expressed ideas. To Elihu the intervention of the Almighty takes precisely the form he had indicated, see xxiii. 19-22, *ante*. He has been disturbed by the dissemination of darkness, and comes to see who is making the disturbance. To Ayub He appears as his vindicator against the world.

3. *Corner-stone;* this is so ancient a rendering, and connects the word with so many passages of the last importance, that it is impossible to think it mistaken. Still the obvious meaning of the word is FACE-STONE, and what follows may be best understood by turning to the daily papers and reading the account of the laying of the so-called *Foundation-stone* of any important building; the said stone not being in the foundations at all, but in the face of the building, visible to all, and bearing an inscription recording the event which it memorialises.

In the present case the reference is evidently to the Great Pyramid, and the FACE-STONE of the Great Pyramid is evidently the HEAD-STONE OF THE CORNER or ANGLE, which capped the whole Pyramid and completed it.

5. Hast thou since thy day commanded the Dawn? The Dayspring will assuredly know his place; to seize control over the wings of the Earth. Then the turbulent will be shaken out of her. She will turn like sealing clay, and they will range themselves like clothing; and their light will be cut off from the turbulent, and the high hand will be broken.

6. Hast thou reached the spring of the Sea, or walked the abysses of Ocean? Have the terrors of Death been laid bare before thee; or hast thou seen the horrors of the shadow of death?

7. Hast thou arrived at the breadth of the Earth? Tell me all about it if thou knowest.

8. Where is this: The road where Light can settle? and Darkness, where is her abode? So that you may take her to her limits, and discern the tracks of her house. Dost thou know it because thou wast then born, and from the record of thy multiplied days?

9. Hast thou come upon the stores of snow, or seen the treasured hail; which I have hidden till the time of the enemy, for a day of battle and war?

10. Where is this: The way Light gleams, and the East breaks upon the Earth? Who clove a channel for the Flood, and a way for the Thunderbolt to rain upon the earth?

---

6. *Terrors, horrors;* the same word in the Hebrew. The ordinary rendering *gates* is equally legitimate, but fails to convey the idea of *dread,* which the same word differently pointed expresses. LXX. endeavoured to express both meanings: ἀνοίγονται δὲ σοι φόβῳ πύλαι θανάτου, πυλωροὶ δὲ ᾅδου ἰδόντες σε ἔπτηξαν. In the former verse also the Greek rendering is noteworthy, namely, with reference to the Dayspring. There is no question of *causing* the Dayspring *to know.* The verb is in Piel, which is intensive of Kal, not causative. The Dayspring *will have no doubt.* So LXX: Ἑωσφόρος δὲ εἶδε τὴν ἑαυτοῦ τάξιν.

Not man spoke the word; Adam had no part in it. To satiate Tempest and Destruction, and to cause a fountain of hope to gush forth.

11. Has the rain a father! Or, who has impregnated the storehouses of the dew?

12. From whose womb goes forth the hail, and who causes the vault of heaven to produce it? The waters transform themselves into stone, and freeze together in the open sky.

13. Wilt thou forge bonds for the Pleiades; or loose Canopus from the yoke?

10. *To cause . . . gush forth;* this is doubtless a poetical rendering, but none the less seems to give the sense in English better than a more literal one. *To cause a growth of greenness to spring up* would be more literal, the figure intended being that the Deluge caused a growth of refreshing greenness, just as a thunderstorm clears the air and stimulates natural vegetation. Green is symbolic of hope, and the symbolism of colour plays an important part in prophetic language.

12. *The hail;* there can be little doubt that this is the intention, and the passage must be rendered accordingly. "Hoar frost" seems to be a mere guess of puzzled translators, the word means *to bend, be hollow cover,* and indeed the last word is almost identical with it in sound; and the following from Shakespeare's "Winter's Tale" may give the clue:

"Is this nothing?
Why, then the world, and all that's in't, is nothing;
The covering sky is nothing; Bohemia nothing;
My wife is nothing; nor nothing have these nothings,
If this be nothing." Act i. sc. 2.

The formation of hail is, indeed, one of the most mysterious of phenomena. Natural philosophy can give no account of it that will bear examination. Unless, indeed, it be considered sufficient to say that it is in some way due to electricity; but this seems to be tantamount to saying that no one understands it.

To translate a word meaning *the deep* by *open sky* may seem a liberty to those who imagine that "the covering sky is nothing," or who forget Who is speaking.

14. Wilt thou bring forth the signs of the Zodiac in their order? And the Wain and her daughters, wilt thou lead them?

15. Dost thou know the ordinances of heaven? Wilt thou establish their dominion upon the earth? Wilt thou raise thy voice to the cloud, and will abundance of waters cover thee? Wilt thou send forth lightnings, and will they go? Will they say to thee, Here we are?

16. Who set wisdom in the inward parts, or who gave understanding to the brain? Who will devise a means to count the sand? Or who will stay the pitchers of heaven, when the dust is melted into mud, and cleaves together in clods?

17. Wilt thou hunt prey for the Lion, or satisfy the

---

13. *Canopus.* There seems little doubt that the *Cluster* refers to the Pleiades. About Canopus there is less certainty, but the analogy of the passage indicates that some Giant among the single stars is intended. Here the word is in the singular; in Isaiah xiii. 10, it occurs in the plural.

To *loose from the yoke* seems better in English than the more literal *undo his traces* or *tractors*, viz., those by which he holds in their orbits his attendant planets.

14. *The Wain and her daughters;* the constellation we call the " Bear" should rather be the *Bier*, if the analogy of the Eastern languages is any guide. *Wain* is rather the English equivalent, meaning the trapezium of the con-stellation, which it should be observed precedes the three stars we call the tail of the Bear or Plough. These three stars are still known in Arabic as *the daughters* of the Wain or Bier, if Gesenius is to be believed.

Massaroth seem certainly identifiable with the twelve signs of the Zodiac, and it seems absurd to keep the word in an English translation.

16. *Brain:* is here used in English as the recognised seat and organ of per-ception and intellect. The Hebrew word has been differently explained, but does not seem applicable to any particular organ.

Pitchers seem better than "bottles," which is apt to suggest a glass bottle; whereas the Hebrew word means a *water-skin.*

souls of the shaggy? For they sink down in their lairs, they sit in their coverts and lie in wait.

18. Who sends to the Raven her prey? For her offspring will cry to God for help; they will wander about till they need food.

19. Dost thou know the time of birth of the rock-loving Ibex? Wilt thou watch the deer when they are breeding? Wilt thou count the months they fulfil, and know when their young will be born?

20. They will bow themselves in travail; they will cast forth their young and end their pangs. Their offspring will wax vigorous, they will grow up in the open; they will go forth and will not return to them.

21. Who sent forth the wild ass free; and who loosed the untamed from the yoke? To whom I have appointed the desert for a stable, and the salt land his quarters. He will scorn the hubbub of the town; the clamour of the driver he will not attend to. The recesses of the mountain are his pasture, and he will tramp after every green spot.

---

17. *The shaggy;* not a "young" lion, but a *shaggy* one, *i.e.*, one who has come to maturity, and grown his mane and all his hair. Gesenius points out the clue, but, as in some other cases, never seems to have fully caught it himself, at least with reference to this passage. The point of the question, with regard both to the lion and the raven, seems to be that they do not use their strength and activity to hunt their prey, but merely to seize it when it is within their grasp; and that they learn to do this only under stress of hunger. In short the beasts of prey have no trace of the *human* (!!) idea of sport, and only kill other animals apparently under the adverse conditions which have resulted through man's abdication of his headship over the earth.

21. *The desert for a stable;* *i.e.*, he does without one.

Tramp after; the intention seems to be that his home is the desert, because he shuns the haunts of men; consequently he is obliged to tramp long distances in search of pasture, and notes the places where he can go to feed.

22.   Will the Gemsbok care to be thy drudge? Will he
spend the night at thy stall? Wilt thou break in Single-
born to harness; will he subdue the valleys after thee?
Wilt thou confide in him because his strength is great, and
leave to him thy labour? Wilt thou trust him to bring in
thy produce, and gather it to thy threshing floor?

23.   The wing of song-birds exults; will the feathers and
pinions of the pious ostrich do the like? For she will leave
her eggs to the earth, and hatch them upon the dust; and
forgets that the foot will press, and the beast of the field
trample. She is hardened against her offspring and disowns
them; she labours fruitlessly, and yet she has no fear. For
God has stilled for her the voice of wisdom, and has given

22. *Gemsbok, Single-horn;* the same word in the Hebrew, which is still
extant in Arabic, and according to Gesenius is applied to the *Oryx,* of which
the Gemsbok is a variety, which seems to suit the context very well. *Single-
horn* is used as an alternative word in deference to the LXX., who render it by
μονόκερως, which they would hardly have done without some reason, and the
descriptions of Pliny, as well as of more modern writers, of a horse-like
animal with a single horn, leave little doubt that such an animal did exist if it
does not now; and the descriptions depict an animal whose characteristics are
eminently apposite to the context. See Rosenmüller's *Morgenland.* Gesenius
thinks that the buffalo is meant, but his " buffalo " is evidently something very
different to the buffalo common in India, where it is domesticated and singularly
slow and ungainly in its demeanour; although it is said that a herd of them
will hunt away a tiger if he intrudes upon them. Schleusner, however, who is
generally a very safe guide, states that μονόκερως was so named not from having
but one horn, but because his horns were not branched like a stag's nor
pronged like the chamois,' nor broad like those of the elk, but straight and
undivided.

23. *Ostrich;* this word is supplied in order that the English reader may
follow the line of thought more readily. No specific bird is named in either
case, but the context shews that *the pious* means the ostrich or some other bird
of like habits.

Song-birds; the noun is a perfectly general one to which Gesenius assigns
the meaning *shouting for joy.* It is in the plural, and any attempt to ignore
this fact leads to hopeless confusion. The sequence of thought seems quite

her no share in understanding. For when from above he plies the lash, he is laughing at the horse and his rider.

24. Didst thou give to the horse his courage? Didst thou clothe his neck with terror? Wilt thou make him jump like a grasshopper? The way he snorts when he is fresh is a caution.

25. They may dig deep, but he will leap over; he will rush eagerly to the clash of steel. He will laugh at fear, and will not give way; he will not turn from the edge of the sword. Upon his prancings dance the quiver, the flame of the spear and the javelin. Amid tumult and commotion he will devour the ground; and he will not believe it is the sound

---

simple and apposite to the context, and might be paraphrased, "The lark will soar and sing over its nest, but the instincts of the ostrich are different, and she shews her piety in a different way."

That the Arabs call the ostrich impious precisely on this very score of her neglect of her young might be a reason against this rendering IF THE SPEAKER WERE AN ARAB. What would be unnatural in a song-bird, which has the gift of joyous song in which to pour forth its gratitude, is not so in the Ostrich, which can neither soar nor sing; and the Almighty sees deeper than man and knows her heart; and finds her, it would seem, the more pious of the two.

23. *When from above he plies the lash;* this seems certainly to be the intention, and much more satisfactory than the usual rendering. Not that the latter is wholly wrong, for there is doubtless an allusion to the swiftness of the ostrich, and the way she uses her wings to help her along; but clearly the ostrich does not "lift herself on high" at all in a physical sense. How far she enjoys the joke does not seem to be stated, but the SPEAKER seems to say very distinctly that HE DOES. And then as if to make amends to the horse He expatiates on his magnificent mettle and courage.

25. *Clothe his neck with terror;* those who do not understand this, nor see how appropriate it is, know nothing of the horse—or they have no sense of humour.

They may dig deep; all translators here seem to overlook the point that the verb is in the *plural* and strictly impersonal, "On creusera bien-avant dans la terre, et il sautera par-dessus."

The clash of steel; or more exactly *the meeting of weapons.*

of the trumpet. Every time the trumpet sounds he will say Yoicks! and will snuff the fray from afar, the raging of the captains and the din of battle.

26. Is it by thine understanding that the hawk hovers, spreading out his wings to the South wind? Or will the vulture mount at thy bidding, and make her nest on high? The precipice is her abode, and she hangs on the fang and snare of the rock. There she will feel the sting of hunger, from afar her eye will make search; and her brood will guzzle blood, and where the wounded fall there is she.

27. And Jehovah answered Ayub, and said: He who impeaches a mighty one is a censor. One who criticises God shall answer it.

25. If this description of the horse's courage seems exaggerated, let the reader call to mind Tennyson's "Charge of the Light Brigade"; and let him remember that it is simple historic fact. Told no doubt in stirring language but without exaggeration; it is because the language is appropriate that it is stirring. If he imagines that the horses concerned did not know what they were doing every bit as well as the men he is vastly mistaken.

Yoicks; is hardly a satisfactory rendering of the Hebrew, but the English alphabet can hardly emulate the expressive monosyllable. For what can be done in English the reader must turn to English authors. The following may serve as a sample:—

> Come if you dare! Our trumpets sound;
> Come if you dare! Our foes rebound.
> We come, we come, we come, we come,
> Says the double, double, double beat of the thundering drum.
> Now they charge on amain;
> Now they rally again.
> The gods from above the mad labour behold,
> And pity mankind who will perish for gold.

26. *The fang and snare of the rock;* if any one wants to know what this means, he is advised to get Mark Twain's works, and look up all passages referring to blue jays, and read them carefully.

Guzzle blood; the lexicon does not help one much to a suitable word here. There is a story that in one impression of A.V., *liked* was printed in mistake for *licked up,* in I. Kings xxii. 38. If a word could be found to combine both senses, that would probably be the word to use.

XXV. AND AYUB ANSWERED JEHOVAH and said: Lo, I am nothing. How shall I answer Thee? I have laid my hand upon my mouth. Once have I spoken, and I will not answer; ay, twice, and I will not add to my words.

2. And Jehovah answered Ayub from amid tempest, and said: Gird now thy loins like a man. I will question thee, and do thou shew Me. Wilt thou further break My judgment? Wilt thou condemn Me that thou mayest be righteous?

3. Hast thou an arm like God, and wilt thou thunder with a voice like His? Display now majesty and dignity, and clothe thee with splendour and pride. Dart abroad the outpourings of thine anger, and see every one who exalts himself and abase him.

4. See every one who exalts himself, and make him bow the knee; and tread down the disorderly under them. Hide them in the dust together; bind their faces in oblivion. And I, too, will confess to thee that thy right hand can deliver thee.

1. *I have laid*; the word is in the *past* tense, which the R.V. so far recognises as to discard the future, by which previous translators have generally rendered it. Ayub is evidently referring to the attitude he took up at the close of his last speech, see xx. 40, *ante*, which all the provocation of Elihu's speech had not induced him to abandon. This may seem a very bold, or even presumptuous, course; but how else is Ayub to disclaim all intention of criticising God?

2. *Wilt thou . . . . be righteous?* This is the usual rendering, and seems quite legitimate; but another seems also possible; viz.: *Wilt thou make me out evil by dint of saying, Thou art righteous?*

3. *Pride*; the root meaning of the word is *to be large, swollen, tumid*; precisely, therefore the idea contained in the colloquial word *swell*, applied to a man of wealth and taste by those deficient in both.

4. *Under them;* apparently meaning under the orderly and submissive, who have bowed the knee, unless it is to be taken impersonally.

5. See now Behemoth, whom I created like thee, he will eat grass like an ox. See now! His might is in his loins, and his power in the hardness of his heart. The tail he brandishes is like a cedar tree; the fear he inspires protects him like a coat of mail. His bones are tubes of copper, and his hide like hammered iron. He is the beginning of the way of God. He who formed him can lay him low.

6. Like rain the mountains will go astray after him, and all the life of the field will smile upon him there. Under the flags he will lie down, he will hide among the reeds of the

5. *In the hardness of his heart;* this seems to be the meaning. The word rendered *heart* means strictly "womb, belly," apparently as typical of the *sensitiveness* of the inner man rather than of the digestive organs. Perhaps *bosom* might give the idea in part, but the English way of expressing it seems rather as in the text.

The fear he inspires; the word rendered "stones" in A.V. and "thighs" in R.V., means really *fear, terror;* and "his fear" means not that he feels, but that he inspires. See the word in Gesenius' Lexicon.

Like rain the mountains will go astray after him; apparently meaning that he will attract the mountains as the mountains gather the clouds, a bold simile, doubtless, but let us see what it may mean. *Mountains* are the prophetic symbol of *kingdoms.* Behemoth then will attract the notice of the kingdoms of the earth. Can it be that Israel after the flesh is intended? And that his hiding under the flags means his taking shelter under the flags of the kings of the earth? And his hiding among the reeds of the marsh points to his sojourn in Egypt? Certainly the Nile affords excellent examples of the *wastes of the river*, and the hippopotamus a type in the animal kingdom which leaves little to be desired.

6. *Hide;* Gesenius renders it "bone," but does not connect this meaning satisfactorily with the root, which means *to cut off.* All the passages he quotes suggest the idea of *stripping, skinning*, rather than of *boning.* Moreover, there seems no reason for supposing that "bars" of iron are intended; the root means to *hammer, forge*, and the distinction drawn is evidently that between hammered or wrought iron and cast iron.

How many interpretations this Divine enigma may have it would be presumptuous to pretend to say. Meanwhile, it is instructive to note that, taking the language in its most literal sense, we have here in Hebrew no inapt description of the steam-engine as adapted to pumping mines.

marsh. The flags will surround him and shelter him, the wastes of the river will encompass him. Lo, the river may rage, but he will not blench, so long as the stream breaks over his mouth. He will survey it, and take it in a net; he will bore its nostril.

7. Wilt thou catch Leviathan with a hook, and still his tongue with a line? Wilt thou put a halter about his nose, and reeve a ring in his cheek? Will he multiply supplications to thee, will he make soft speeches to thee? Will he make a covenant with thee, wilt thou take him for thy slave for ever? Wilt thou smile upon him as on a bird, and bind him for thy maidens? Will the Hebrews chaffer over him; will they distribute him among the Canaanites? Wilt thou fill his hide with harpoons, or his head with the clatter of fish?

6. *The stream; Jordan* seems to mean *Ford* or *Fords*, and so any stream. *So long as it breaks over his mouth;* i.e., so long as it is deep enough to swim in. There cannot be too much water for him, all he has to fear is lest the stream should fail. *He will take it in a net;* i.e., the fish will catch the fisherman, so to speak; *bore its nostril, i.e.,* subdue it as a man does an ox. This is the way LXX. understood it: ἐν τῷ ὀφθαλμῷ αὐτοῦ δέξεται αὐτόν, ἐνσκολιευόμενος τρήσει ῥῖνα. Which is as close as anything can well be, and the whole passage seems to be wonderfully descriptive of the way Israel after the flesh treated Pharaoh and the Egyptians of old, and have treated kings and nations ever since.

7. *Hebrews;* or more exactly *Heberites,* which probably means the same thing, at least where chaffering over a bargain is concerned. The alternative meaning, however, may well be noted, *Will the associations dig pits for him, will they part him among the fisher-folk;* the Canaanites or Phœnicians being the sailors, traders, fishermen, of the Mediterranean.

Harpoons; this seems pretty well accepted. Leviathan is not to be slaughtered like a whale; what whaler would dare to attack the sea serpent?

Clatter of fish; this also seems to be pretty plainly expressed; "fish-spears" lacks authority completely, and is a mere guess of puzzled translators. What precisely is meant it is perhaps difficult to say; but why does the salmon take the fisherman's bait? The arrangement in crimson and gold which is dangled before him is like no known genus of fly, and, moreover, the salmon is not on the feed when in fresh water.

Lay thine hand upon him!! Think of the contest. Thou wilt proceed no further. Lo, to wait for him will only bring disappointment. Nay, will not the sight of him overthrow? I am not talking at random, for he will rouse himself, and who is there will stand before him?

8. Who has forced himself into My presence, and been dismissed in safety? Under all the heavens it is thus. Did not ꓲ decree his separation, and the word of his power, and the fascination of his nature?

9. Who has removed the garment that veils him? Who has ventured to wear his bridle? Who has opened the door of his presence chamber? On every side he is girt with terror, majesty, a channel of shields, an enclosure of sealed rock. Each joins each and wind may not penetrate within them.

10. Man shall cleave to his brother; they shall grow together and shall not be separated. His sneezing will cause light to shine, and his eyes are as the opening dawn. From his mouth go forth torches; fiery hammers escape. From his nostrils proceeds smoke as from a steaming cauldron

---

9. *Who has removed the garment that veils him?* Compare what Ayub himself had said about Leviathan, iii. 2, *ante*. *Ventured to wear his bridle;* this seems pretty plainly expressed; more exactly: *Who has come within the doubling of his bridle?* JEHOVAH as it were points out to Ayub some of the horses in HIS stable.

10. *His eyes are as the opening dawn;* or more exactly *as the eyelids of dawn:* What says the Scripture? "Verily, verily I say to thee: Until one is born from above he cannot see the Reign of God, Jno. iii. 3. The imagery of this book of Ayub has puzzled all translators, but then translators appear never to have read the best literature in the library of man. Compare for instance the account of the birth of Noah in the book of Enoch, written before the Flood, and the description of the birth of Sigurdr the Wolsung, in William Morris's English version of the old Norse Niblung legend.

when the fire is blown. His breath kindles coals, and flame issues from his mouth. In his neck dwelleth strength, and at his presence languor will dance.

11. The flakes of his flesh adhere firmly; they are rigid upon him, not to be shaken. His heart is firm as a rock, rigid as the nether millstone. When he arises the gods will give way; they will be broken and miss their road.

12. The sword that moves against him shall not stand, the spear, the dart, and the coat of mail. He will count iron as straw, and copper as rotten wood. The arrow shall not make him flee; sling-stones are changed into chaff for him. A club is reckoned as a reed, and he will laugh at the brandishing of a spear.

13. His bed !—Lance-points; he will spread sharp stones on the clay. He will make the depths to boil like a cauldron, he will use the sea as a pot of ointment. After him will gleam a track; he will make the waves like hoary hair. There is not a similitude for him on earth for unscrupulous

10. *Languor;* Gesenius says "terror," but in this he contradicts his own account of the word, from a root meaning *to melt away, pine, languish*; and misreads the whole intention. LXX. render very well, ἔμπροσθεν αὐτοῦ τρέχει ἀπώλεια.

11. *The flakes of his flesh;* this gives the physical side only, the thing signified seems to be the *weaknesses, failings*, of the flesh. So St. Paul says, "When I am weak, then am I strong."

13. *His bed lance points:* so LXX. evidently understood the passage: ἡ στρωμνὴ αὐτοῦ ὀβελίσκοι ὀξεῖς, and this is supported by the following clause. The point is that the sufferings of man are self-inflicted; no instruction and no experience seems to teach him to behave sensibly and rationally, and so he misses the blessing God would bestow.

The depths; here evidently the abysses of ether, as in many other passages. It should be remembered that man is the subject of this description, and, indeed, the whole intent of the book seems to be to shew man to himself as the heaven-abiders see him.

work. He will see every height. Who but he is king over all the sons of pride?

14. And Ayub replied to Jehovah, and said: I see that Thou canst do anything; and craft can withhold Thee no jot. Who will hide counsel thus without knowledge? Therefore my words were mere gush, and I have no discern- ment. Far be distinction from me; and I know nothing.

15. Hear, I pray Thee, and I will speak; I will ask of Thee, and do Thou instruct me. I had heard of Thee with my ears, and now my eye has seen Thee; wherefore I abhor myself, and lament in dust and ashes.

XXVI. AND IT CAME TO PASS, AFTER JEHOVAH had spoken these words to Ayub, Jehovah spoke also to Eliphaz the Temanite: My anger is kindled against thee and against thy two companions, because they did not utter sincerity to Me like My slave Ayub.

2. And now, take you seven bullocks and seven rams; and go to My slave Ayub, and offer them as a burnt-offering to testify to you. And Ayub My slave shall make inter- cession on your behalf—for lo, I lift up his countenance—lest I do you a mischief; for you have not uttered sincerity to Me, like My slave Ayub.

14. *Without knowledge, i.e.,* unless he knows. It was said of an able am- bassador that he could hold his tongue in seven languages. When the sons of Adam learn to control the tongue, to use and not abuse it, they will be far on the road to manhood.

But the Hebrew is double-edged, and may equally mean, "Who is so absurd as to hide counsel by sheer ignorance." Ayub thus, in one sentence, justifies his Maker, and confesses his own weakness.

3. And Eliphaz the Temanite, and Bildad the Shuhite, and Zophar the Naamathite, went and did according as Jehovah said to them. And Jehovah lifted up the face of Ayub, and Jehovah turned the captivity of Ayub, when he made intercession in testimony to his companions.

4. And Jehovah added all that Ayub had twice over. And there came all his brethren, and all his sisters, and all who had known him before; and all bred with him in his house.

5. And they condoled with him, and comforted him, over all the evil which Jehovah had brought upon him. And they gave him each, one kesita and one ring of gold.

6. And Jehovah blessed the after-life of Ayub more than his beginning; and he had fourteen thousand sheep, and six thousand camels, and a thousand yoke of oxen, and a thousand she-asses.

7. And he had seven sons and three daughters. And he called the name of the first Jemima, and the name of the second Keziah, and the name of the third Keren-happuch.

---

5. *Kesita;* a word not often used and of uncertain meaning. Gesenius shews some grounds for thinking it to be the name of a certain standard of weight equal to about four shekels, and the analogy of the passage strongly favours the idea that a certain weight of silver is intended. Compare Gen. xxxiii. 19, with Gen. xxiii. 16. In the former the word *kesita* occurs, in the latter shekels; and if, as seems probable, the sum paid was about the same in each case. . . .

7. *Jemima;* or Dove. *Kesiah,* or Cassia. *Keren-Happuch;* One who brandishes her horn. Gesenius says, " horn of paint," but gives no explanation, nor does there seem to be any etymological reason for supposing that Ayub gave so senseless a name to his youngest daughter. She was probably a wilful miss, as youngest children are apt to be, and somewhat given to tossing her head ; and appropriately named accordingly.

And no women were found so fair as the daughters of Ayub in all the land; and their father gave them property among their brothers.

8. And Ayub lived, after this, one hundred and forty years; and saw his sons and his sons' sons, four generations. And Ayub died an old man and full of days.

THE WHOLE BOOK OF AYUB.

8. *The whole book of Ayub;* or *Ayub wrote the whole.* In the Hebrew there are three words only. If brevity be the soul of wit, then there is wit without stint in the book. The vocabulary in Hebrew is limited, but those who knew how to use it made it sufficient to express a great variety of ideas.

At the end of Deuteronomy stands a single word, meaning HOLD FAST.